Maye. '22

T.

Stephen Burgen

DaLoRu Books

Published by DaLoRu Books

Designed by Georgina Rosquelles
Cover photo by Susan Ridge

ISBN: 978-84-09-44495-3

Printed in Spain by Qpprint, Barcelona

For Sarah, obviously

Contents

Acknowledgements
7

The Jacket
9

The School
31

Motherland
65

Epiphany
81

Victor
105

Kiss
127

348 Grosvenor
153

Ladies' Man
189

Ima
211

Due Diligence
231

Wasted ad Wounded
253

Acknowledgements

For their encouragement and general *ánimo*, especial thanks to Jane Darroch Riley, Scott Riley, Mary Davison, Ryan Chandler, Sharon Cuzens, Katherine Bonner, Sarah Shaw, Fairlight Books, Alex Warner, Judy Thomson, Kirsty Gunn, Meaghan Delahunt, Gráinne Lyons, Phillippa Warner, Gina Rosquelles and, of course, Sarah Davison.

The Jacket

All my priceless things are but a post the passing dogs defile.
W. B. Yeats

It took a moment for Michael to realise that it was his doorbell that was ringing. He wasn't expecting a visitor or a parcel and it was weeks now since any flowers had been delivered. His first reaction was dread. He was too raw and fragile to deal with anything or anyone unfamiliar. He even struggled to cope with the man who came to read the electricity meter. To a stranger, Michael looked normal, melancholy perhaps, but normal. They'd have no idea how thin the ice was. He needed to carry a warning, a sign that read: Fragile. Handle with care. He'd considered getting a T-shirt printed with the word Bereaved but people would probably think it was a band or a TV series. The doorbell rang again, drawing him out of that faraway nothing nowhere place where mourning had taken him of late, a vacant space defined by absence. From the outside, he appeared lost in thought, but if anyone asked him what he was thinking he'd confess he had no idea, he wasn't thinking anything, he was just bobbing around on a sea of loss, a small vessel cut loose from its moorings, adrift in a dreamless reverie.

He didn't recognise the face of the youngish, fair-haired man on the small videophone screen.

Is that you, Mike?

Mike. Some people called him Mike, generally people who think if they go straight to the diminutive it sounds more friendly. But anyone who really knew him knew he didn't ever go by Mike. The figure in the street stood back from the camera, hands on hips, impatient to be let in. Michael didn't know who he was but there was something familiar about him that he couldn't place.

I'm sorry, he said. Do I know you?

It's Erik.

He didn't know anyone called Erik. Thieves were always scamming their way into the building, posing as plumbers or Amazon or the phone company. After the last robbery, videophones were installed and everyone in the building had been warned: unless you can positively identify someone, don't let them in. Erik was a stranger and even if he wasn't a thief, dealing with strangers was on the longish list of things that Michael could still barely handle. With strangers, sooner or later you have to account for yourself, and he wasn't ready for that yet. If people didn't know what had happened, he didn't have the strength to tell them. He'd only start crying and he was a bit sick of crying. He needed protection, shielding, like someone with compromised immunity, except in his case it wasn't opportunistic infections he feared; it was raw, unscheduled contact with strangers.

I'm sorry, I can't let you in if I don't know you.

The figure flapped his arms, annoyed or frustrated or both. He carried a plastic carrier bag in one hand.

Michael studied the face on the screen. Had he known him once? He didn't think so. He wouldn't say he never forgot a face; he forgot a lot of things. What he did forget was where he knew people from. He'd say hi to someone in the street and then spend the rest of the morning struggling to remember who they were. Sometimes it was just context. Like when he passed the woman from the chicken stall in the street, he knew he knew her but because she wasn't quartering chickens in a bloodstained apron, he couldn't remember from where.

Maybe you've got the wrong address, he said into the machine.

The Erik person shook his head slowly from side to side, almost sorrowfully.

I'm a friend of Leo's.

Michael caught his breath, the shock of Leo's name on this stranger's lips. Erik could have said any other name and he wouldn't have let him into the building, but he said Leo and it was like an incantation. At the sound of his name something rose within him, like a guttering candle flickering back to life, something very like hope.

He pressed the buzzer. Through the speaker he heard the click of the door releasing and saw Erik enter the building. He opened the apartment door and listened to the lift descend to the ground floor, the door open and close, the whine of the mechanism as the lift rose up the shaft. It stopped on his floor, the doors parted and out stepped a man of medium height with short fair hair and bright blue eyes, a scrub of blond beard, and a scar along one eyebrow, like a boxer. He felt certain he'd never seen him before in his life.

There was a little too much zeal in Erik's eyes, something knowing, like someone who's been touched by a guru or is living a post-revelatory life. But there was something else, a shiftiness, edgy, both furtive and vaguely menacing. He felt himself recoil, suddenly aware that he had invited this stranger in and acutely conscious of his inability to handle the simple niceties of social interaction.

Erik waited, one hand on the door frame, a shade too proprietorial, and flicked his eyes towards the interior of the apartment, as if to say, aren't you going to invite me in? Michael looked at him blankly. Unable to process this person in the doorway, he'd retreated back to the nowhere place where he kept disappearing, from others and from himself, a suspension of time and space, his own private petit mal. Then he snapped back to the present, standing in the hallway, one hand on the door, the stranger asking to be let in.

His instincts told him no. He should just say sorry, you must be mistaken, we don't know each other, and close the door, except that Erik said Leo's name. He imagined Erik as a messenger of sorts. But there was something else that stopped him shutting the door in his face. He was dressed in jeans, red Reeboks, a black T-shirt and a midnight blue leather jacket. It was the jacket that was familiar.

He stepped aside by way of invitation. Erik embraced him lightly, or not so much an embrace as a hand gripping each shoulder.

I'm sorry for your loss, he said. He had an accent, Dutch or Scandinavian.

He accepted the condolence as he had so many of late, numbly, and not as graciously as he would have wished. He nodded by way of thanks. He'd stopped saying thank you for people's sympathetic words, not that he wasn't grateful, but it felt unnecessary. That and the fact he had so little to give, even thanks. He'd been hollowed out by loss, stranded in an emotional void.

There was scarcely room for both of them in the cramped hallway. He stepped away so that Erik could close the door. He led Erik past the kitchen where Michael hesitated. Should he offer him coffee, a beer? If he did, and Erik accepted, then he would stay, and he didn't think if he wanted him to. He continued on into the small living room and gestured towards a chair. Before he sat down, Erik looked around the room, as though appraising the contents for auction or as a would-be tenant or buyer might.

Nice speakers, he said as he sat down, smoothing the plastic bag on his lap. The bag was from the duty free at Schiphol airport.

Wharfedales, Michael said without expression.

Erik made no response and continued to check out the room, his eyes roaming along the bookshelves, taking in the jazz festival poster, the family photographs, some in colour, some black and white, the ceramic evil eye brought from Istanbul, the Murano glass fish, wilting white lilies in a vase, the sympathy cards on the mantlepiece that Michael didn't know how or when to take down, the view out of the window on to next door's washing.

Everyone listens on headphones these days but I like ambient sound. Maybe I'm old fashioned.

Erik raised an eyebrow.

The speakers, he explained.

Oh, right, said Erik. You're a big Mahler fan, right? Not really my cup of tea, Mahler.

Erik continued his appraisal, this time of Michael, who he held in his blue, aloof gaze. His lashes and eyebrows were blond, like Boris Becker, Michael thought. He was annoyed with himself. Why did he say that about the speakers? Why tell him anything about himself? And how did he know that about Mahler? All he wanted to know was what Erik had to say about Leo. After that he could go.

So, how are you managing, Mike?

Mike again. Where did he get the idea of calling him Mike? Not from Leo, that was for sure. He let it go. He shrugged.

It must have been tough, the loss. And so sudden.

Wrong tense, he thought. Is tough, not must have been.

I hear you've been kind of depressed.

Hear from who? he said, suddenly defensive. From whom? He corrected himself, instantly annoyed by this futile pedantry.

You know, around, Erik said, with a wave of his hand that took in the world at large.

The leather creaked as Erik raised his arm.

Grief unpicks logic, things unravel and resist order and connection. Even when it's obvious that the stranger sitting opposite you is wearing a leather jacket that until recently belonged to you, it doesn't make sense. Grief blocks out the obvious conclusion, that somehow, by fair means or foul, this person has acquired your quite recently stolen jacket. It wasn't his imagination. Erik was wearing his jacket. It wasn't that it was exactly the same as his jacket, it was his. How could that be and what did it mean?

Michael didn't care much about clothes, but he loved that jacket. It was Leo who had talked him into buying it. They were on holiday in Palermo and they'd just had a long lunch, so long the shops were opening again for the evening. They were wandering around, going nowhere in particular, following their feet, feeling free and easy, full of calamari and wine and limoncello, when they passed a shop with the jacket in the window. They'd stopped to admire it. It was a plain leather jacket, that was its appeal. Michael liked clean lines and hated garments adorned with superfluous zips and studs and straps. The jacket was elegant in its simplicity. But it was the colour that got their attention, a deep, midnight blue. Leo pulled him towards the shop doorway.

Come on, try it on. I want to see you in it.

He resisted but Leo had tugged at his arm.

You don't have to buy it, just try it on.

Leo had that way about him, he turned everything into a bit of a dare. He was always chivvying Michael along, teasing him out of his comfort zone, pushing against his shyness. The shop assistant was young, haughty and camp. He'd gushed all over Leo while flagrantly ignoring Michael. Leo flirted with the shop assistant. He liked to flirt, just for sport, he said. He was so much surer of himself than Michael. Leo explained with extravagant gestures and three words of Italian that Michael wanted to try on the jacket. The assistant gave Michael an up and down, like a farmer assessing livestock at auction, clearly not impressed with what he saw. He flicked through the rail and handed Michael a jacket. He'd put it on, shyly, intending to take it off immediately and hand it back and hustle Leo out of the store. But the leather was so soft, the lining silk, or silky at least. He'd never experienced anything like it with a piece of clothing. It was like a second skin, second but better. The moment he put it on he felt transformed, complete. He felt ready.

You look great, Leo said. It's perfect. You should buy it, shouldn't he, he said to the assistant, who nodded while making a moue that said he thought the jacket was wasted on Michael.

Quanto? Michael asked.

The assistant wrote the price on a scrap of paper, assuming Michael either wouldn't understand if he told him or couldn't possibly afford it. It was a lot of money, far more than he would ever spend on clothes. Leo and the assistant both stood with their arms folded.

Go on, Leo said. Spoil yourself for once. You know you love it.

Later that evening they'd had an argument, more of a spat really. Maybe it was the lunchtime drinking gone sour, though the jacket seemed to have something to do with it. Michael made a jokey comment about Leo flirting but Leo took it the wrong way and the evening ended badly, with neither of them speaking. They made it up later, after he apologised and Leo, who resorted to his preferred weapon – a chilly silence – accepted his apologies and relented.

And now here was this Erik, who claimed to know Leo, wearing Michael's jacket.

Where do you know Leo from? he said, with unintended hostility.

Oh, you know, from the circuit. The first time we met was at the Berlin festival. After that we kept running into each other.

So you worked with him?

Yes and no. Basically I'm a facilitator. We're in the same business but doing different jobs. Were, I should say. I still haven't got used to thinking about Leo in the past tense.

Michael's throat tightened whenever someone said Leo's name, like it was stuck there. He hadn't yet used the past tense either. Leo was still in limbo between here and there, here and gone. He laced and unlaced his fingers and waited to hear more from Erik. It was only since he died that he realised how many other people there were in Leo's life and how many lives he touched. He didn't belong to Michael, or not just to him.

The last time I saw him was in Amsterdam. There was some cock-up with a hotel reservation so I put him up at my place.

This was news to Michael.

When was that?

I don't remember exactly, a while back.

Funny, I don't think he ever mentioned you.

That's not surprising, Erik said. He often talked about you, though.

Often? So you saw a lot of each other?

He was curious to know what Leo said about him, but he wasn't sure he wanted to hear it from Erik.

Like I said, we were both on the festival circuit. It's a small world.

Was Erik trying to tell him that there had been something between him and Leo? He searched his memory for any mention of Erik. The search came up blank. Leo was away a lot; it went with the job. His and Michael's working lives didn't overlap. There were a lot of people in their lives they didn't have in common, which they agreed was a good thing, that they didn't live in each other's pockets, but it was also a source of friction. Leo's life was more glamorous than his, or so he thought; he felt excluded and a little bit jealous but struggled not to show it.

One day, when Leo was going to Bruges for a few days for work, he suggested that he tag along.

I've always wanted to go to Bruges, he said. I won't get in the way. I'll do my own thing, go to galleries, whatever, and then when you're not working we can have a little holiday together.

It doesn't really work like that. I think you have a picture of these trips as a sort of junket, an excuse to have fun while someone else is paying, but it's not like that. It's work and I hardly get any down time at all.

Oh, go on. You could find time for dinner, surely. That's all. I know you'll be busy, but it would be fun.

I don't think it's a good idea.

He was hurt that Leo so clearly didn't want him spilling over into his working life.

Anyone would think you're ashamed of being seen with me, he said archly. He regretted it. Leo had no time for petulance. Any moment now and he'd call him a princess, one of his favourite put-downs.

You're being silly now, he said.

Oh, silly is it? he said, still more petulant, his voice rising a couple of tones, aware that he was digging a hole for himself but unable to stop. Silly to want to spend more time with you.

Leo sighed and plucked a piece of lint from his sweater.

We spend a huge amount of time together, he said, a little coldly, the emphasis on huge implying it was already more than enough.

It's OK, Michael said, backing off testily. Don't worry, I won't cramp your style.

What's that supposed to mean, cramp my style?

You're so secretive, that's all. It makes me wonder what you have to hide.

I'm not secretive. I just don't think we have to share every single second of our lives. It's not healthy. Everyone needs a bit of space. You can be so … so smothering sometimes.

Smothering! he exclaimed sarcastically. Well, god forbid. Give the man some air. Let him breathe.

Oh, please, Michael. This is so childish.

Once again Leo retreated into silence, though with him silence felt more like an offensive than a withdrawal. Back when they first met, he never imagined Leo would go for him. Leo was vivacious, flirtatious and self-assured. He was arty, and though not an artist himself he moved in those circles, organising festivals and concerts. Michael's job in human resources was better paid but not nearly as glamorous. He was naturally shy, hesitant and unsure of himself. Leo loved to dance but had to cajole Michael on to the dance floor. Leo moved with a cool naturalness as though the music flowed through him while he had to concentrate to keep the beat and learnt his moves from a video.

Yet Leo wooed him, not that it took much wooing, and what began as a fling became a thing and, had Leo not died suddenly, they would soon have celebrated their twenty-fifth anniversary. In love, the die is cast early on and calibrates the mood for what is to follow. So all along Michael felt lucky – unexpectedly lucky – to have Leo, not that Leo, who adored him, didn't appreciate his own good fortune. The difference was he believed Michael was nothing more nor less than he deserved whereas Michael never lost the sensation that he was loving beyond his means and that, like all imposters, he would one day be found out.

Leo's death changed all that, leaving him dwarfed by the enormity of what might have been, with the end of possibilities, not with all they had done together, but everything they would never now do. He wanted news of Leo, which was why he let Erik in, because he said he knew Leo, and to Michael that made him an emissary, like the bit part player in Shakespeare who arrives with news from afar of the protagonist's wife or his ships. He wanted to hear anything that would keep him among the living – stories, anecdotes – hearing tales of Leo helped to stave off the cold, implacable fact of his death. But he wasn't sure he wanted to hear Erik's stories. There was something odd about him, something wrong, false even. And he was wearing his leather jacket.

It was the theft of the jacket that had pushed him over the edge, not that it took much. After Leo's death he scarcely left the house. The outside world was too raw and his skin was too thin. He took nothing in his stride. Even the quotidian miseries of the city clawed at him, the desperate and unhappy people who weren't getting and weren't going to get the help they needed. Like the young man who lived on a ledge below a cash machine. His world had been reduced to this small space. He sat there by day and slept there at night. He probably wasn't much more than thirty although in six months he'd aged five years. He rarely spoke except to acknowledge the hand that dropped a coin into his cup. On a piece of cardboard propped against the ledge he'd written: I was like you once and one day you too could be like me. Leo called him the ancient mariner.

One day his friend Carmen coaxed him into going out for a drink. Carmen was in for the long run. He sensed that other friends were already weary or repelled by his grief and thought it was time he got over it, time he was moving on. Someone had even uttered the word closure, for god's sake. But Carmen was prepared to sit it out and let him take his time. She didn't tell him what he ought to do or how he should feel.

It was a warm, sunny day in late October and they were in a bar outside on the terrace. Michael draped the leather jacket over the back of his chair. He managed some conversation in between the petit mal absences that punctuated his day like power cuts. Suddenly, an argument broke out nearby, two men, raised voices. Then, as suddenly as it started, the dispute was over and the two men vanished. That's when he discovered his jacket was missing. The argument had been staged, a distraction, while the accomplice made off with his jacket. It was an old trick.

As soon as they realised what had happened everyone got up and looked around in case the thief was still in sight but of course he wasn't. Michael's mood passed from anger at himself for being so stupid and for falling into the trap, when everyone knew never to leave a bag or a jacket on the back of a chair in this city, to a deepening despair that spread through his being like a stain. Just when he was beginning to haul himself up off the canvas, the theft had knocked him back down. It rammed home his feeling of powerlessness and the inability to exercise control over his life. The waiter came over and gave him a lecture he really didn't need about leaving things on the backs of chairs. Carmen took him back home to the sanctuary of the sofa. She made him tea. She sat with him until he gave her permission to leave.

You can go, he said. I'm OK.

Except he wasn't. The grief that confronted him, already insurmountably vast, a Himalaya of sorrow, now engulfed him entirely. The mantra that he repeated to himself, that he had a duty to Leo to live, that he must find the strength to go on because that's what Leo would have wanted, began to recede and fade like a train pulling away into the night. He slid from mourning into depression, neither wishing to die nor eager to live.

He couldn't put the loss of the jacket behind him and continued to relive the moment of the theft. The thought of it filled him with impotent rage. He would lie in bed, fists clenched, enacting and re-enacting violent fantasies of what he would do if he ever caught the thief. It wasn't just the jacket. The jacket was special, it made him feel good to wear it, and it was a memento of him and Leo and Palermo, all of that mattered. But what really got to him was knowing that he'd been had, he'd fallen for the trick like some dumb tourist. The theft had nothing at all to do with Leo's death but in his mind the two coalesced, even though one loss was so much greater than the other. He said to Carmen: I feel like everything I've ever wanted, everything I've treasured, is being taken from me. Carmen gave him a hug and he wept into her luxuriant hair.

Since then he had gone out for a few short walks, though never unaccompanied, and had seen hardly anyone until Erik arrived at his door. Erik studied him with a sympathetic look that Michael was beginning to feel was completely fake. He began to feel that Erik was one of those people who is always performing, who has learnt to seem the way Michael learnt to dance; all surface, no content, a performative human being.

I really should get going, Erik said. I really came here to give to give you this, he said, patting the plastic bag on his lap. It's Leo's, a shirt that he left in my apartment. I thought you might want it.

Erik made it sound so natural, too natural, that Leo would leave a shirt behind in the apartment of a man whom Leo had neglected to mention, even though Leo did sometimes talk about his work and the people he worked with, usually if he had a funny anecdote to tell or if someone was being especially difficult or annoying. Evidently Erik was neither amusing nor annoying enough to merit a mention.

Erik held the bag towards him. Michael hesitated. Accepting it seemed to imply accepting more than the return of Leo's shirt. It implied that Erik had occupied a place of some, if minor, importance in Leo's life. It felt like collusion. He took the bag from Erik and held it for a moment before he looked inside. The moment he opened it the scent, the indefinable, unmistakeable scent of the living Leo, wafted out. More than any words or photographs or memories, that lingering trace of life overwhelmed him with the knowledge of what was lost. He held the shirt up to his face and began to weep in great heaving sobs, soaking the shirt with his tears.

Erik didn't get out of his chair. He didn't put a consoling hand on his shoulder. Michael was relieved; he could do with some consolation, but not from Erik. As the sobbing subsided, he folded the shirt and slid it back into the bag. The two of them sat in silence. Erik could go now, as far as he was concerned. He'd done what he came to do which, along with returning the shirt, was presumably to put thoughts into his head that he'd rather not have, to make him feel bad or foolish or naïve. Perhaps sensing this, Erik got to his feet.

I should go, he said.

Michael nodded.

Where did you get that jacket? he said.

This? I bought it here in one of those vintage shops. Why?

It's mine.

Erik laughed. It was more of a snigger, sardonic, disbelieving.

Yeah, right.

Really, I'm not kidding. It was stolen a few weeks ago. It's my jacket.

I don't think so. Maybe you had one like it.

His tone was sarcastic now, and aggressive. Erik's charm, such as it was, slid behind a cloud.

I'm not accusing you; I don't think you stole it. I imagine it's just a bizarre coincidence, but it's mine and I want it back.

Are you serious? I mean, really? Leo said you could be a bit of a head case but this is really off the wall. It's my jacket. I probably still have the receipt somewhere.

That stung. What did Leo mean, he was a bit of a head case, and why would he tell Erik that? In what context? He felt betrayed by Leo, if he really did say it, and now there was no way of asking him if it was true. If what Erik really wanted was to stick the knife in, there was nothing he could do to stop him.

Why did you come here?

I told you why, to return Leo's shirt. And to offer my sympathy.

But why did you really come?

Jesus, I really don't need this, Erik said, moving towards the door. Michael stood in the narrow doorway. He held his hand up.

The jacket, he said. You may well have a receipt. I already said I don't think you stole it, but even if you bought it in good faith, the jacket is still rightfully mine.

You're out of your mind.

Maybe so. Look inside. The label says Cusumano, Palermo, and there's an ink stain on the lining, on the inside pocket in the shape of a heart, or a spade, if you like. Go on, take a look.

Erik's face hardened. Slowly he opened the jacket, and there was the heart-shaped stain on the lining, and above it the label: Cusumano, Palermo.

You see, he said. Erik eyed him coldly.

I reported the theft to the police, he lied. I could call them now and say you have turned up wearing it.

That doesn't prove I stole it, which I didn't.

No, it doesn't. But it could be awkward, couldn't it? Tedious, at the very least. I could make a fuss. The police might decide that here was one case they could clear up for a change.

He could see that Erik was weighing it up. He felt empowered for the first time in months. Erik narrowed his eyes, then removed his wallet from one pocket and his keys from another. He took the jacket off and held it towards him on the end of his index finger, as though it were something distasteful that he'd rather not touch. Michael took it from him, slid open the deadlock on the apartment door, then closed it without a word to the departing Erik.

He sat at the kitchen table until darkness fell. He scarcely ever drank but he took out the Macallan, Leo's favourite whisky, and poured a couple of fingers into a Waterford crystal tumbler. Leo wouldn't drink whisky out of any other glass. He was particular about things: the correct glass for red or white wine, demi-tasses for coffee, a cheese knife for cheese; not fussy but particular. He held the glass up to the light, the way Leo did, examining the golden liquid refracted through the faceted glass. He set it down beside a framed photograph of Leo. The picture was taken on the small ferry to Ithaca. Leo wore a half smile, his face was tanned, his arms dark against a loose white shirt. He looked immortal.

Someone named Erik called by today, he said to the photograph. Or that's who he said he was. He said you used to work together, or not together exactly, but you knew each other through work. He brought me your shirt, the apple green one we used to call your Granny Smith shirt. I don't know what he was doing with it. He said you'd left it in his apartment, which seems strange. I don't know whether to believe him. The funny thing is, he was wearing my leather jacket, remember, the one I bought when we were in Palermo. It was stolen a few weeks back. I didn't tell you at the time; I was afraid what you would say, like what was I thinking leaving anything on the back of a chair in this town.

It seemed like a sign, Erik wearing the jacket, though I don't know of what. Just a weird coincidence, I suppose. I don't think you would have liked him, he was a bit creepy and sort of supercilious. The sort who thinks they're better than everyone else, or smarter. Bit of a dick, frankly. Just for once I was glad you weren't here because he's just the sort of guy who presses your buttons. You probably would have told him where to get off. Now that he's gone, I realise none of it makes any sense. Why did he have your shirt? Why was he wearing my jacket? He kept calling me Mike, like we were old pals, but you know no one calls me that. There are a hundred questions I should have asked him but I can't think straight. Sometimes I really feel like I'm losing my mind.

But the shirt is definitely yours, Leo; it still smells of you. I didn't really think you had a particular smell, though I guess everyone does, and I didn't know I missed your smell till now. But then there isn't anything I don't miss about you. I keep finding out more things, more ways that you are absent. It's like when your house has been robbed and for weeks afterwards you keep finding things missing. I didn't like Erik, but what I really didn't like was that he had your shirt. It made me wonder if I'd missed something, failed to see the signs. Was I blind? Love blinds – that's what you used to say, love blinds. Maybe it does.

Every night for the past six months when he talked to the photograph, he ended up crying, but this time the tears didn't come. He turned the photograph face down on the table and finished the whisky. The jacket hung on the back of the chair. Reclaiming the jacket was like making good on the lesser of his losses, not the one that really mattered. It was just a jacket, not a triumph over adversity, not one he'd got over Erik. He knew he'd never wear it again. It had lost its allure and would forever be associated with, and tainted by, Erik.

He picked up his keys. The gaunt homeless man was in situ on the ledge by the bank. Michael handed him the jacket. He took it and rubbed the leather between his thumb and forefinger, assessing it quality, but made no comment.

It's Italian, Michael said, foolishly, as though that mattered.

He didn't try the jacket on. He lay it on the ledge beside the rolled up sleeping bag and the flattened cardboard boxes. He held up the paper cup and rattled the few small coins it held. Michael patted his pockets and shrugged apologetically.

I'm sorry, he said. I've nothing on me, then looked away rather than face the man's look of contempt and disappointment.

He sat in the dark at the kitchen table. Since Leo's death he felt diminished. Losing Leo felt like losing so much more than him. He had lost the sense of himself, at sea with no compass and no idea which way the land lay. He felt like he'd been cheated because Leo had been cheated out of what should have been the rest of his life. He'd have done anything for that not to be true, for Leo to come back, no questions asked, no need to explain; and they could just carry on as before like nothing had happened. But that was before Erik arrived with the shirt. That changed things; in a way, it changed everything. The jacket, that could just be a weird coincidence, but not the shirt.

It wasn't that he chose not to believe that Leo and Erik had been lovers, he simply chose not to think about it at all. All the same, something had shifted. What felt impossible, unthinkable even, drifted within reach, like a ship emerging from fog. He felt released from the burden of believing that seeking or even stumbling upon a moment of joy amounted to betrayal; that to be happy in Leo's absence would be proof of his unfathomable shallowness. As the fog lifted, he saw a way back into the world. He had been paralysed by grief and loss, unable to see a way forward or back. His life had been on pause. The mere fact of being alive felt wrong, leaving him no option but to shut himself away and grieve. But

Erik's visit, distasteful though it was, had opened the door. He had permission and he had choices; he could choose life.

The School

I don't belong here, I really don't, but I have mouths to feed, which is how I've ended up doing communications for a business school run by Catholic fanatics. Most days I feel like someone in a witness protection program, living in constant fear that my cover will be blown and I'll be exposed, the Christ killer lurking in the garden of Gethsemane. But it's a job and we're in a recession caused, in part, by what is taught in just this sort of institution.

It may sound odd that an organisation modelled on Harvard Business School should be run by religious fanatics but this is Spain where the two top business schools are run by, respectively, the Jesuits and Opus Dei. It makes sense. The good old god-fearing days when church and state were hand in glove have passed. Modern Spain is a godless democracy where women are allowed to hold bank accounts and no one raises an eyebrow at abominations like same-sex marriage. The church has lost its grip over the nation's morals.

The thinking that drives the sect behind The School – it has another, fancier name but everyone calls it The School - is as follows: the centres of power have shifted and the church needs to keep up. It needs to ensure that good, Catholic men are at the heart of where the action is, which is in business and politics. As a strategy, it's exactly the same as Trotskyist entryism; installing right-thinking people in strategic positions where they can discreetly influence policy and spread the word.

I am personally involved in promoting a world view – capitalism is great, god is greater – that I don't share. But until something better comes along, say, a job in an atheist cooperative that pays as well as this, I try to stop beating myself up about it.

My assignment today is to interview Unai Echevarría, an Olympic silver medallist and, more importantly, an ambassador for The School and its values. I was at the gate of his mansion when my boss Anna called. Anna is my immediate boss – power is so diffuse at The School I could name any number of people as my boss – but she's the one I answer to. As soon as I'm out of sight, Anna calls. She's mistrustful and always wants to know where I am, as though if she took her eye off me for a moment I'd be propping up a bar or lying on the beach.

What's up? I said, looking up at Unai's house, a big pile concealed behind high walls and big gates. It could have been Belgravia or Bel Air. The wealthy all live in the same house. Later, after Unai's fall from grace, the press always referred to the house as a *palacete*, a little palace. I spoke my name and business into the video-phone at the gate. A buzzer went and the gate swung slowly open.

I'm revising your piece about Sebastià Roig, Anna said.

Is there a problem?

It's the headline.
You don't like it?
Me da miedo.

The first time Anna said *me da miedo* – it scares me - I took it literally. But what she means is it makes me nervous because I don't get it. Which means she is worried someone else, ultimately the dean, won't get it. But the dean wouldn't admit he didn't get it, because that would make him look foolish. Instead he'd say something opaque like, maybe you should rethink the headline, without giving any indication of how, leaving Anna – and me – to guess why he didn't like it and what sort of headline he would prefer.

A word about the dean. Like other top members of the faculty, he is one of the *illuminati*, as sect members are known, and lives a monkish existence. He's cadaverous, from fasting and mortifying the flesh. The School isn't a happy place and there seems to be little joy in doing god's work, but the dean's bloodless face and scrawny neck call out for someone to sit him down to a plate of lasagne and a full-bodied red, maybe a Barolo or Malbec. He wears suits from El Corte Inglés that hang on his bony frame so that he looks like a refugee outfitted by the UNHCR. He walks with a stoop and avoids eye contact with anyone below a certain rank. He speaks little, as though words, too, are an indulgence. I have rarely known a man so uncomfortable in his own body, but then if you live in fear of nightly visits from a succubus, your body is not your friend.

I can't talk now, Anna, I said. Let's talk about it when I get back.

The Olympian – he won his medal for archery, a rich man's sport - was an alumnus of The School and I was there to get some quotes out of him about how The School had turned his life around. It was that sort of job. It was common knowledge that Unai was as dim as an English winter and it was whispered that he never completed his MBA and only graduated on the understanding that he would use his fame to promote The School.

Besides, the real reason Echevarría was famous wasn't the silver medal, it was his wife, the wonderfully named Lucía Santamaría De Havilland Escajedo. Lucía was a staple of *Hola!* and for years had been living off her fifteen minutes of fame as a young soap star. Her acting days were behind her but she was also the king's cousin and in line to be the duchess of somewhere, heir to a title and little else. More hat than land, as they say in Texas. Before settling on Unai she had a series of what the popular press liked to call tempestuous, but in any case, highly public affairs with others who, like her, were it not for *Hola!*, would wither away from lack of exposure.

Lucía was also a regular on *tertulias*, that peculiarly Spanish species of chat show, ostensibly a round-table discussion but in reality a pontificating contest in which the person with the loudest voice and the least inclination to listen prevails. *Tertulias* are populated by has-beens, people who were famous once or were married to someone who was once famous: C-list actors, ageing cabaret and soap stars, failed Eurovision competitors, retired bullfighters, retired bullfighters' former wives, men with badly-dyed comb-overs, women with colossal hair, false eyelashes and kilos of make-up and - to add a pinch of gravitas – at least one washed-up journalist, drawn from that tribe of sclerotic men of a certain age who clog up the arteries of informed debate, men with a tendency to launch their prolix ramblings with a dangling participle lest they commit themselves to anything coherent.

I was shown into Unai's palace by a young woman dressed in the sort of dark suit worn by hotel receptionists. She led me into an entrance hall that was bigger than my living room. She invited me to wait, gesturing to a red leather, button-backed, gilded chair. I sat there, obliged to face my reflection in an oval, gilt-framed mirror. After about ten minutes a man in his forties with immaculately-cut greying hair arrived. He wore an expensive but unfashionably cut suit, a pale pink shirt and a blue and pink striped tie. There's a certain type of posh Spaniard who send their children to English public schools and whose idea of style is to dress as badly as the British royal family. This was one of them.

I'm Javier, Señor Echevarría's personal assistant, he said, shaking my hand with little enthusiasm.

He led me down a corridor to a small sitting room, where I was again asked to wait. I'm used to this, it's a routine among the rich and famous, hiring people to handle the nuts and bolts of life, layers of protection. It sends out the message that they're tremendously busy with important matters and haven't time for such trivia as greeting their guests or opening doors. And as a journalist, I knew that Unai was making me wait to remind me how unimportant I am, not that I need reminding.

Everything about the room contrived to convey old money and class but it was clearly fake – from the leather-bound books on the shelves to the paintings of naval battles. Perhaps it was Unai's idea of himself, but it had been executed by an interior designer working to a brief. There was a Miró above the mantelpiece. It caught my eye, as it seemed out of place with the rest of the décor. When I took a closer look, I discovered it was an original; you could see the brush strokes.

I was examining it when in walked Unai. It's a cliché that when you meet famous people in real life they're always shorter than you imagined, but Unai was taller than I expected. Tall and bone thin, like a distance runner, which he wasn't, with the hollow cheeks and haunted look of someone who's done a lot of time, which he hadn't, or not yet. He offered me a firm handshake and a thin smile and gestured for me to sit in one of the brocade armchairs.

So, fire away, he said, easing his long body into the armchair. Even sitting down he was tall.

I was there to talk to Unai, as he was popularly known, and about his company, wittily named Unaite. Unaite was in the business of introducing people who have interesting ideas but no money to people with more money than they know what to do with for each other's mutual benefit. Its latest venture was to establish training centres to find useful tasks for the idle hands of the nation's youth, about half of whom were currently unemployed.

Well, Señor Echevarría, I said.

Please, call me Unai.

This appeal to familiarity was at odds with the look he gave me, which was devoid of any expression. He wasn't cold, it wasn't that; when I looked into his eyes, they were empty.

OK, Unai, let's talk about this new venture, the youth training centres. How did it come about?

And so off he went. The patter was rehearsed, slick. He was good at the corporate social impact talk, though rather light on detail. When I asked where the centres were located and when enrolment would begin, he looked past me to a point just above my head, as though searching for the information.

I'll have to get back to you on that, he said, having failed to locate what he was looking for. Better still, Javier can get you that information, he said with a wave of his hand that suggested details were what underlings are for.

Unai's eyes told me he had no interest whatsoever in talking to me and was only here out of a sense of duty to The School. That was fine by me; I hadn't come to make friends. And while I would, of course, write about this admirable venture, the real point of the interview – of every interview – was to get the subject to say something nice about The School. It wasn't journalism, it was advertising. Whatever the subject at hand, the real topic was The School and its mission. It prided itself that 95 per cent of graduates were earning six-figure salaries within three months of completing their MBA, although if you could afford the fees you probably didn't need money. But despite the huge fees The School was always short of cash and my job was to remind these lucky graduates that The School had given them a leg up and now it was time to put their hand in their pocket.

There was an unspoken understanding between me and my subjects that in the course of the interview they would say what a life-changing experience their time at The School had been. Ideally, they would say the experience was transformative, a word much loved by The School, as though paying a hundred grand for an MBA guaranteed you a Damascene epiphany. A good interviewee would conclude with how The School had imbued them with values that they were now building on to make the world a better place. One thing I discovered from these encounters was that it was possible to make the world a better place even while pursuing a career in such unpromising fields as private banking and reinsurance.

Most of the people I interviewed were fairly dull and unknown outside their field of operations. What they said wouldn't go beyond the quarterly alumni magazine which, as far as I could tell, no one read anyway. But Unai was a celebrity which meant the interview would be tweeted and maybe picked up by mainstream media. So, it was time to nudge Unai towards saying how The School had changed his life.

Tell me about your time at The School. What sort of impact did it have on you?

Extraordinary. Immense. Life-changing.

I nodded appreciatively.

Transformative, he said.

Good boy, I thought. Before he could elaborate on this we were distracted by raised voices outside and we both turned to the window. It was Unai's wife, Lucía. She was talking in a loud voice to Javier. She looked distressed. Javier put out an arm to stop her but she waved him aside and suddenly there she was in the doorway.

She was dressed casually in a teal shirt and jeans but made up as though for the camera. Unlike her husband, she was shorter than I imagined and not as pretty as she looked on TV, maybe because on TV she was always smiling. She wasn't smiling now. She had a hard face, not unlike her husband's; hard and embittered.

Hi, Lucía, what's up? Unai said.

She looked at me. Unai, confused, extended his arm in my direction as though about to introduce me, except he'd forgotten my name. But she didn't care who I was. She looked her husband in the eye and uttered the dreaded phrase: we need to talk.

Unai's frown deepened and he pursed his thin lips until they all but disappeared. He inclined his head to Javier who in turn inclined his towards me. I nodded slowly, completing this piece of silent male communication. I got the message; my time was up.

My apologies, Unai said. I hope you've got enough for your article.

Yes, I think so, which of course I hadn't; we'd hardly got going. Thank you for your time. It would be great if you could arrange to send some photos to illustrate the piece.

You can deal with that, can't you Javier? he said.

Of course, Javier said with little conviction. I'll see to it.

I said my goodbyes. Unai wished me well and I drew a barely aspirated *adiós* from Lucía.

Without actually touching me, Javier hustled me along the corridor, shook my hand and all but pushed me through the gate.

Don't forget the photos, I said, but he'd already turned his back.

When I got back to the office I could see right away that Anna was in a mood. She didn't say anything and didn't have to; like a chilly sun, Anna could radiate froideur. Even at the height of summer she could chill the office with a sidelong glance. I chose to overlook it and gave her an excessively cheery hello which she acknowledged with a millimetric tilt of her chin. She wasn't one to relinquish a bad mood without a fight. I imagined her throwing a sulk at home. Husband: what's the matter? Anna: if you have to ask there's clearly no point me telling you. That kind.

How was Unai the mighty bowman? Cesc asked.

Tall, I said. Unexpectedly tall.

There were four of us in the office: Anna, Cesc, Meritxell and me. Between us we produced the magazine, the internal online news and the blog. We tweeted anything we thought might be of interest to the wider world. Everything went out in Spanish and English. English was my domain.

And did you meet the lovely Lucía?

Not exactly, but she was there.

And how is the nation's darling in real life?

Short, hard and very angry about something, but one shouldn't go on first impressions.

Is that blogpost ready? Anna said from behind her screen.

Working on it, Cesc said, throwing me a wink. He had the Ticketmaster site up on his screen. He was always going to gigs. Cesc got a kick out of taunting Anna by blatantly failing to do what she asked, knowing she couldn't sack him because he was protected from on high. He was connected. His father was an alumnus and was known to have made a hefty donation to The School, which made Cesc untouchable. Although still in his twenties, he appeared to have no ambition beyond doing as little as possible. I'm not sure I knew what his job was, but then that was true of a lot of people who worked at The School.

If Anna disliked Cesc, it was nothing compared to her contempt for Meritxell, the hopelessly incompetent production editor. When I came in, Meritxell was hunched over her keyboard, wrapped as she was in all seasons in layers of wool and a voluminous scarf. She would have been chilly in hell. Her beloved highlight pens were lined up beside her keyboard. She had a mania for drawing up work-flow charts and then colouring them in to show how much she had achieved, which in reality was precious little. Like most incompetents, she never took the blame for anything. It was always someone else, the software, the photographer – there's someone like that in every organization.

Given Anna's contempt for Meritxell and Cesc's contempt for Anna, I was, by default, the boss's favourite. Nevertheless, she viewed me with suspicion and could smell my disaffection. Even so, she treated me with a degree of deference. Why? Because I knew her secret. She was having an affair. I'd never have guessed, because she's such a devoted wife and mother. The only non-work conversations I have with her are about our kids and her husband. But if there's one thing life has taught me it's that, however well you think you know someone, there is always something you never imagined, something surprising. Everyone has secrets and Anna's secret was that she was having an affair with Pablo Sagrera, The School's professor of corporate social responsibility. Sagrera wasn't one of the *illuminati*, but his wife, who worked in The School's admissions department, was deeply religious and wore a large gold crucifix – not just a cross, a crucifix – around her neck.

It happened like this. One day after work I'd got almost all the way to the metro station when I realised I'd left my mobile at work. I dragged myself back up the hill and when I opened the office door there were Anna and Sagrera. They were fully clothed, they weren't even touching. They stood close together, both affecting the strained nonchalance of people caught en flagrante delicto. A second before I opened the door they were kissing. I knew that because the shape of where they'd just been, in each other's arms, remained, as though sculpted in the air, like a ghost. I saw it and they knew I did.

I picked up my mobile and looked her in the eye.

Sorry to interrupt, I said, with what was perhaps a gratuitously malevolent smile.

Ever since then I have carried this secret with me like a lucky charm and, without saying as such, have made it clear to Anna that her secret is safe with me. But it gave me something you can never have too much of - leverage. Leverage is one of the words you hear a lot in business schools, but they're talking about profits whereas what I had in mind was blackmail.

Anna was paranoid, not about her affair, well, that too, but the place oozed paranoia. The School's attempt to reconcile godliness and Christian ethics with grasping, rapacious neo-liberal capitalism resulted in it being like an ethical version of the Hadron collider. How to square heartless, profit-driven capitalism with Jesus and the moneychangers and the twenty pieces of silver? The School's assertion that capitalism is a force – indeed, the force – for good was proving difficult once the financial crash had revealed the gaping hole where ethics were supposed to be.

Now it was confronted with numerous and egregious cases of unethical behaviour – Madoff, Freddie Mae, Enron, Lehman Brothers - it was a long list. How did The School deal with this apparent contradiction? It didn't. It pretended none of this had happened. These cases weren't mentioned and they weren't used as case studies. If anything, they were nothing more than bad apples in a righteous barrel. When a deputy dean of Harvard Business School told me in an interview that much of the blame for what had happened lay with what was taught at business schools such as his own, Anna deleted the comment from my copy before it got as far as our own dean, to whom such home truths were secular blasphemy.

There was a sense of unreality about the way issues were debated. One afternoon, for example, I was sent to cover a discussion about how to do business ethically in countries where bribery and corruption are the norm. The countries cited were in Africa, Latin America and the Middle East. This was at precisely the moment when almost every day a Spanish politician was indicted for corruption and people were discovering what they'd long suspected, that the entire political class was a self-serving, nepotistic kleptocracy. There were at least a dozen Spanish students at the talk. I looked around thinking, come on one of you, there's an elephant here in this room, speak up. But not one of them thought – or dared – to question the state of business ethics in their own country. They knew: if the professors or the invited speakers don't mention it, probably best not to bring it up.

This atmosphere of paranoia also created decision-making phobia. Everyone avoided making a decision, in case it was the wrong one. If a decision had to be made it was referred up or sideways or else someone would call a meeting. Everyone was second-guessing their superiors, all the way up to the cadaverous and uncommunicative dean, who no doubt was looking over his shoulder to the board of governors, the bishop, the Vatican and probably to *el señor* himself. The School preached openness and lean management but practised something more like Soviet bureaucracy.

I didn't know why Anna was in a mood and I wasn't about to ask. Nor was I going to ask what she didn't like about the headline I'd written for the article about Sebastià Roig. I put on my headphones and started transcribing what little I'd got out of Unai Echevarría. About twenty minutes later she sent me an email, although she was sitting a few feet away. When you're ready, can we talk about Roig, it read. Rather than reply I went and stood behind her. She had the story up on her screen.

She tapped the screen. The headline read: It's a family affair.

You don't like it?

Me da miedo.

She turned to look at me. Anna had an angular face and mousy hair but she had the most beautiful eyes, neither brown nor green, but at once amber and jade. And like a lot of Spanish women, she had sexy eyebrows. If you don't know why or how eyebrows can be sexy, I can't help you.

I could see the problem, or rather, I could see what she saw as a problem, but I played dumb.

What don't you like?

It's the word affair. People might think …

And there it was. Would a native English speaker think a family affair had anything to do with trysts, dalliances or affairs of the heart? Would their sexual innuendo alarm go off? I don't think so. But Anna was second-guessing the dean, the same dean who once pulled a photo of a female student because she was wearing jeans. Who pulled another photo of people toasting with champagne glasses despite the fact that one of the big cava houses was a patron of The School. Who crossed out the words intimately related in copy and replaced them with closely related.

I had been employed with specific instructions to liven up the magazine, the headlines in particular. The trouble is, a good headline often involves a play on words. Anna spoke English, as did the dean and everyone else she answered to, but they weren't native speakers and didn't speak it well enough to appreciate wordplay. Consequently, she/they worried that any playfulness might detract from the seriousness of the article – The School wasn't big on laughs – or worse, might conceal some mocking or subversive meaning. So, on the one hand, Anna was grateful to me for exerting quality control on The School's English, most of which was written by non-natives. But she also feared that I might slip something irreverent past her just for my own amusement, for which she would take the rap. I can't deny that I was often tempted.

It's not a bad headline, I said. It's not great but it does the job. It tells the story.

The problem was that the story was boring. All of our stories were boring, crushingly so. But, however unappealing the story, the headline has a duty to go out and pimp for it.

The headline's job is to say: read me, I said.

Anna nodded, but not in agreement. The School lived in mortal terror of controversy and Anna ensured the magazine didn't contain any. The result was bland, insipid and dull. But dull was good; no one complained about dull. Besides, as I said, no one read it. I pictured it landing on executive desks all over the world until, still in its plastic wrapper, it was quietly binned.

How about Family Values? I said.

That's better, she said. Don't you think so?

No, I didn't, but it didn't really matter what I thought, nor did I care that much. The headline wasn't a hill worth dying on. Nothing I did there was. But I understood why Anna was freaking out: Sebastià Roig was a member of the sect, one of the *illuminati*. Most of the people who worked there were, like me and Anna, civilians, but there were *illuminati* in every department, like spies. They never openly proclaimed themselves, just as The School was never open about being run by religious fanatics, although it was public knowledge.

Not many of the women were *illuminati*, but the ones that were or had married into the sect, were easy to spot because they never had fewer than four children. Spotting the men was less straightforward but the main clue was that no one seemed to know why they were there or what if any their area of responsibility was. They had job titles and their own offices and secretaries, but their function was obscure. Most *illuminati* didn't live a monkish existence, they were out there in the world of politics and business. Sebastià Roig was one of them. He owned a very successful luxury goods business. The School had no beef with luxury.

A funny thing happened at that meeting where Roig was speaking, I said to Anna. I didn't mention it in the piece because you would have cut it.

She made a face.

Funny how?

Of course, the funny thing, as I saw it, was that The School sent a man to give a talk about work-life balance when it's almost always women who have the biggest problem juggling career with family. Anna herself was constantly on the phone doing precisely that, telling her husband or her mother that she had to go to yet another meeting and could they pick up the kids, take them to piano class, cook dinner.

Do you really think, as a woman, that Roig, given that he's a man and what he stands for, is the best choice to lead a discussion on striking a balance between work and family life?

Roig is highly respected, she said.

That was typical Anna. It was typical of The School. Never criticise. Never commit. Never say anything anyone could call you on later. *No te mojes*, as they say in Spanish – don't get wet.

The fact is The School had a problem with women. The people behind it, the sect, believe a woman's place is in the home, making bread and babies. *Kinder, Küche, Kirche*, as the Germans used to say. But half the students are women so they can't come out and say it. You can hardly tell ambitious young women, many of whom have had to fight to get an education in the first place and are now forking out tens of thousands for an MBA, to get back in the kitchen. It would be like trying to reconcile the Middle Ages with #MeToo.

So what did Roig say that was so funny? Anna said.

Oh, it wasn't what he said. He said the usual stuff. I could have written it without showing up. Family values. Values in general though he never said what they were. Being a good citizen and a good mother or father. Moral authority comes from following universal principles, he said, whatever they are. There's no such thing as business ethics, there are just ethics. Same old same old.

Anna frowned. She didn't like my tone. I often suspected she agreed with me but she was never going to let on.

Anyway, I said, Roig was riffing on the old family value stuff when this student raised his hand and said, are family values intrinsically good? Do they necessarily lead to good and ethical behaviour? Of course, they do,

Roig said. Then the student said, what about the Mafia? They're big on family values. What about them?

Oh nice, Cesc piped up. Bullseye. I bet Roig just loved that? What did he say?

He ignored him. He pointed to someone else who had their hand up and moved on. I had to bite my lip to stop from laughing. But the kid wouldn't let it go. Excuse me, he insisted, it's a legitimate question. The Mafia subscribe to precisely the values you describe. How can they be good in one context and bad in another? Roig got all flustered, said the comparison wasn't valid, and then blundered on. Poor kid, I expect his dad will be getting a letter from the dean pretty soon.

Never let anyone outside the family know what you're thinking, Cesc said in a very poor imitation of Marlon Brando.

Anna went back to her screen. She wasn't amused, or if she was, she had to cover up. That was how paranoid the place was.

Are you all set for this evening, she said?

Sure, though I don't get why everyone is so excited.

Well, it's a bit of a coup for The School that Stone is coming to speak to us, Anna said.

Words of wisdom from Mr Coffee, Cesc said.

But he practically went bust, I said.

That's why, said Cesc. Haven't you noticed? Failure is the new success. Fail fast, they all say it.

It was true. Nearly every business leader who spoke at The School made a shibboleth of failure, of how much they'd learnt from failure, how they'd been humbled by it. Failure had been recruited to their militaristic vocabulary of campaigns, frontiers, price wars, pre-emptive strikes and tactical alliances. Fail fast was the new mantra.

Harold Stone, the CEO of the CoffeeTown chain of coffee shops which had only avoided going bust by sacking thousands of staff, was coming to talk to students. For days everyone had been in a state of nervous excitement about his visit. You'd think Moses or Jimi Hendrix had come back from the dead to speak to us, not just the boss of a company that served insipid coffee.

Be sure to tweet, Anna said. The dean asked specifically.

I will. By the way, my Unai copy's a bit thin. We were just getting going when his wife put a stop to things. He was pretty vague, to be honest. I've asked for pictures so we'll have to pad it out with them. You know, happy young people making something of their shitty lives thanks to Unai's inspired scheme.

Always so sarcastic, Anna said.

Ironic, not sarcastic, I said. There's an important difference. Sarcasm is for laughs, irony is about survival.

I had another job before that evening's Harold Stone event which was to interview three MBA students for the alumni magazine. These interviews followed the same pattern and served the same purpose as the interviews with former alumni. The students would say how much they'd got out of the experience, how it had transformed the way they viewed the world and how they were going back out there not only to do well but to do good. Occasionally a student would admit that the other great takeaway – everyone talked about takeaways – was the incredible list of contacts they acquired after spending two years at The School associating with the sons and daughters of the global elite.

The first two interviewees were young men, one from Mexico and one from Washington state. Neither of them had anything interesting to say. I've interviewed dozens of students at The School. They come from all over the world and yet, wherever they are from, for a group of young people they are strikingly uniform. They all say the same things and have the same values. They all use the same jargon as the professors - going forward, reach out, drill down, touch base, leverage, next level. When they talk about eco-systems they mean the business environment. For them the word sustainability has nothing to do with environmental responsibility; by sustainable they mean profitable.

None of them said anything original or controversial, which made me wonder if the spirit of paranoia also permeated the lecture theatres. Even their transformative experiences, which were apparently de rigueur, were interchangeable and store-bought. Whether they were from Shanghai, São Paulo or Cincinnati, male or female, whatever might have once distinguished them from each other had been smoothed away to produce an homogenous, humourless *homo comercio*, a brand of person. Most of them were distinct from each other only in the way that one five-star hotel or first-class airport lounge differs from another.

Oh, and they never talked about money, as though making money was the furthest thing from their mind. In fact, making money was never mentioned at The School. Never. Accruing vast personal and corporate wealth was apparently incidental, a side-effect of capitalism's *primum mobile*, which is to create social wealth and jobs. Despite its Christian ethos, The School frowned on charity. It preferred social entrepreneurship; helping people (at a price) to help themselves. It was the teach a man to fish principle, but the fishing lessons didn't come cheap.

The third interviewee was a blue-eyed, black-haired Iranian woman in her late-twenties called Rafsana. We sat in in a room on the sixth floor overlooking the city. The School was high up on the hill, beyond the reach of public transport, as public transport isn't something people who live up there use. Siting it up there reinforced the message drummed into the students that they were tomorrow's leaders. With the city spread out before you and beyond it, the sparkling Mediterranean, it was easy to imagine you were serving an apprenticeship to become a master of the universe.

Nice view, isn't it? she said. She spoke American English.

Tibi omnia dabo si cadens adoraveris me, I said.

What?

All this can be yours if you will fall down and worship me. It's from the Bible. It was Satan's offer to Christ. He took him up on a hill and said all this is yours if you follow me. Jesus said no, of course.

She gave me a puzzled look with her bright blue eyes.

So, tell me about your time here. How has it been?

Good, really good. But I don't think they really understand how people do business outside of the U.S. and the rest of what we call the West. They think you sit down, talk business and make a deal, she said. But there's hardly anywhere in the world where that's true. It's all about family connections. I live in New York and what I like about it is they take you on face value. People say, I like that idea, we'd like to invest in it. It's the idea they're interested in. If I was at home in Iran they'd want to know who my father is, my uncle, my family. In the U.S. no one cares.

It's the same in Spain, I said. Spain is more like Iran. Connections are everything.

Really?

Sure. If you interview two people for a job and one is your cousin, your cousin gets it. No question. If you don't give the job to your cousin people will want to know why.

What about here?

Here? You mean The School?

Yes. They talk a lot about talent and merit but I'm not so sure. Some of the professors seem, well, pretty ordinary, to be honest.

I wouldn't know, I said, determined not to be drawn into saying something I might regret. The rest of the interview followed the normal course, although I couldn't wheedle the word transformational out of her. I was already wondering if I could use what she said about The School not understanding how business is done in the rest of the world, which was implicitly critical and therefore wouldn't get past Anna.

When we were done, we stood at the window, admiring the view. The sun was going down and the city was bathed in pink light.

Don't you think it's a bit weird, a religious business school? she said.

God and mammon under one roof. That's the School's USP. What's not to like?

I was showing off. I wanted her to like me.

You're funny, she said, but she didn't look amused. I was annoyed with myself. I made it a rule never to express my opinion to anyone except maybe Anna and Cesc. Don't trust anyone: that was my motto at The School.

I got myself to the auditorium half an hour before Stone's talk was due to begin but it was already filling up. I managed to find an aisle seat about ten rows back from the stage in order to escape unnoticed as soon as possible. I set up the tools of my trade – laptop, notebook and pen – checked the WiFi was functioning and lined up some hashtags on a blank document so I could cut and paste Tweets. Someone from communications had already tweeted about how Stone's visit had caused a fever of anticipation at the school.

A steady stream of students and faculty filled the seats. The decor was fawn and grey. The only decoration was a discreet crucifix on one wall. The audience matched the furnishings. The School preached iconoclasm, transformative experiences and thinking outside the box but you'd never guess from the dress code that this was a roomful of people destined to rip up anyone's rule book.

Most of the female students wore business suits, generally grey or navy, with white shirts. Some wore trousers and a few wore jeans, though they were frowned upon. The female faculty dressed the same as the students, though never in jeans, which were contractually forbidden, as were short skirts or showing cleavage.

As for the men, the ocean of grey was broken only by small archipelagos of navy and midnight blue. Shirts ranged from white to pale blue, or white with a faint stripe, with pale pink reserved for the racier or more off-beat faculty members. Most wore ties, either from their old university or else the sort of striped affair favoured by TV sports presenters. The male students were allowed to forego ties – they were young, after all – but were otherwise indistinguishable from their professors. Only a few Latinos wore T-shirts and jeans, along with some Japanese striving for cool, and there were some Americans, usually Californian, whose ripped jeans and raggedy T-shirts aspired to a Silicon Valley credibility.

There was a buzz of excitement in the auditorium, like before a concert or a football match. Jordi, the house photographer, waited at the edge of the stage for Stone to appear. Jordi had been at The School for as long as anyone could remember. He was a nice enough guy but a hopeless photographer. All he had to do was take head shots and cutaways of men in suits either speaking at a podium or, like today, having an onstage armchair chat. Jordi was incompetent, most of his pictures were either out of focus or had some extraneous and distracting detail, or the subject's eyes were shut, but he'd been there forever so he was, in effect, family, and therefore had a job for life.

The auditorium was now standing room only. Anna was there at the back. She didn't need to be there but staff must have been told they were expected to attend. She would have got her mum to look after the kids. We exchanged nods. Stone came on accompanied by the professor who would act as moderator. The techie guy, who had also been there for years and was as bad with microphones as Jordi was with a camera, adjusted their lapel mics in between shrieks of feedback. Stone wore a monogrammed shirt with HS embroidered on the collar. I considered tweeting, Wtf!? Harold Stone wears monogrammed shirts, but thought better of it.

The professor introduced the great man to enthusiastic applause. It was a great privilege to have someone so wonderful and from whom we could learn so much here at The School. In a moment, Harold Stone (the professor pronounced it Hald Estone) would share with us some experiences from his extraordinary career but first a quick look at some of the highlights of his journey towards becoming one of the most successful and innovative businessmen of recent years, the professor said. You'd think it was the Grammys.

We sat through five minutes of glossy video about CoffeeTown which was roundly applauded. Then Stone spoke. He struck a note that was both valedictory and heroic, as though we were gathered together to commemorate a great battle. When he spoke about himself and his achievements, he pulled off a nice line in humble self-aggrandisement.

He said that being the Nº 1 consumer brand on Facebook and Twitter enabled CoffeeTown to build its emotional engagement with its customers. I tweeted that, though I had no idea what it meant, and also tweeted what he said about customers wanting to support those companies whose values are consistent with their own. I held back on his comment that people don't want to work for a company they don't trust and they're not proud of, because I imagine many, perhaps a majority of employees, are not especially proud of their employers, let alone trust them.

The sub-text of all this was that CoffeeTown was a wonderful company, though one that had lost its way. This was something Stone had detected early on in its decline, despite, he insisted with unconvincing modesty, not being smarter than anyone else.

It's not that I was clairvoyant but I had an intuitive sense that the beginning of the end was approaching, he said, demonstrating that he was indeed smarter than everyone else. Straight to Twitter, thank you, Harold. He went on to explain that to ensure this was only the beginning of the end and not the end itself, he was forced to close 800 cafes with the loss of 6,700 jobs.

I stood up in front of the entire company and I apologised. As leaders we have let you and your family down, Stone told the hushed auditorium, tearing up just a tad, before adding: We had to confess.

I glanced over at the dean to see how he was taking this. Catholics are averse to this Baptist sort of public *mea culpa* and prefer to beat themselves up in the privacy of the confessional. The dean was certainly not one to spill over the side. But he sat attentive and expressionless, his hands folded on his lap, like a small boy in the presence of one of his heroes.

Then Stone spoke of the day when he had to deliver the bad news to all those thousands of employees who loved and trusted CoffeeTown, the people whose livelihoods he was about to bring to an abrupt end: It was the worst day of my life. I cried.

I Tweeted that, of course, and then he was done. He got a rapturous standing ovation. The Q&A that followed was even more fawning than usual. Bored, I Googled Stone and discovered his net worth was around $5 billion. I thought it would be good to Tweet that, too, just to put his tears in context, but I have mouths to feed and precious little net worth of my own. I stayed to the end but sat through the final standing ovation, pretending to work. I slipped out when Anna wasn't looking and headed home, relieved to get away from the place.

It was dark by the time I left. I walked down the hill, the city twinkling below me, a few lights at sea of ships waiting to dock. Every day I worked there I said to myself, one day more, one day less. Tomorrow I would write something flattering about Unai Echevarría and I would do the same for Harold Stone, with no mention of his fake humility and his five billion dollar tears, and the dean would like the piece enough not to say anything at all, which meant he liked it, which meant Anna would also be pleased and relieved and so would I because in some childish schoolboy way I wanted to please her and get a pat on the back from teacher with the lovely eyes. But it was bad for me, it was all done in bad faith. The School presented itself as a champion of ethics and decency when the truth was it was a swamp of lies and hypocrisy, moral window dressing for the status quo; power and privilege dressed up as the common good. Not for the first time, I vowed to quit as soon as I could.

The next morning, I planned to work at home. I'd write up Unai and Stone and send them in. Then I'd go in later when Meritxell had made up the pages. I'd been pushing for over a year to persuade Anna to let me work from home. She never said so but I knew she thought I'd just be swinging the lead, sitting around in my underwear watching daytime TV. I argued that she knew I was working because she could see what I produced. There was no sense in my going to the other side of the city and tramping up the hill to do something in an office that I could just as well do at home. I hated the journey to work. The last stretch was up a steep hill and I always arrived soaked with sweat. After a long campaign I won the battle to work from home, but Anna called or messaged constantly, just to keep me on my toes.

My plan to stay home that morning fell apart as soon as I saw the news. Unai Echevarría had been arrested on charges of misuse of public funds, money laundering and tax evasion. His business partner, Pablo Sagrera, professor of corporate social responsibility at The School and Anna's lover, had also been detained on similar charges. I was already on my way in when Anna called.

The media are all over this, she said. We've been told not to speak to anyone.

There were a couple of TV satellite trucks outside the school. Anna looked up and nodded when I arrived, Cesc wore a malicious grin, while Mertixell made a big show of concentrating really hard on what she was doing, like a small child who's been told off by teacher and is trying to get back into her good books, not that there was any way she'd ever win Anna's approval.

When you interviewed him yesterday, did he talk to you about the youth centres, Cesc asked?

Yes, but he was very vague about it.

That's because the scheme is a sham that only exists on paper; there are no youth centres nor is anyone involved in establishing them.

That would explain why he got jumpy when I asked for locations and photos.

Cesc waved me over to look at his screen. He was watching a news stream. There was footage of the police carrying computers and boxes of documents from the house where I'd interviewed him. The reporter outside the house was already calling it a *palacete*.

But look at this. It's unbelievable, he said. He opened The School's intranet and typed Unai Echevarría in the search field. The message came back: no matches found.

Wow! That was quick. He's been wiped.

This parrot is deceased, it has ceased to be, it is an ex-parrot, said a gleeful Cesc, who was a huge Monty Python fan, even though the show must have stopped screening by the time he was born.

I was shocked. Talk about hero to zero. Unai was a tireless ambassador for The School, ready and willing to be wheeled out whenever they needed him to keep it in the news and in the money. But now he was news for all the wrong reasons and The School lost no time in removing every trace of him. Unai was a non-person.

What about Sagrera?

Same thing. Zero mentions. Another dead parrot.

I tried to catch Anna's eye but she didn't look up.

That's pretty scary. What ever happened to innocent until proved guilty? You'd think The School might have waited till they'd had their day in court.

We have a problem, Anna interrupted. Unai was a four-page spread, so now we have a four-page hole. Meritxell is making a new flat plan.

That explained Meritxell's pose of I can't talk now I'm just so incredibly busy. She couldn't draw up a flat plan without tutting and sighing.

So we go big on Mr Coffee Shop?

Exactly. Stone was already four pages, the dean now wants six. I'll run two house ads and then we'll be OK. Can you do that?

Anything to keep you and the dean happy, Anna. You know that. I live to serve.

Anna rolled her eyes.

Here's an idea, Cesc chimed in. We could run mug shots of all the people Stone sacked. That would fill up a load of space, maybe even the whole magazine.

In between writing about Stone I kept checking news sites for more stories about Unai. The media were loving it, of course; everyone loves a fallen idol. Various pieces implied that Unai was greedy but not very bright and that Sagrera was the brains behind the scam. The focus was as much on Lucía as on Unai. She was filmed leaving the house in dark glasses and a headscarf. An indignant looking Javier led her to a waiting car. I looked over to see what Cesc was up to. He was booking tickets to a Supertramp concert.

Meritxell finally finished the layout and I sent her my text to input. It came up short so I stretched it out with crossheads and pull quotes. When I was done, I closed the file and told Anna I was going home.

I think you should stay, she said.

Why?

She didn't answer. Instead she sent me a WhatsApp.

We have a problem, it read.

Another one?

Yes, a comment you made about The School. It got back to Núria.

Núria was Anna's boss.

Really, what did I do?

I told you, it was something you said.

We were sitting opposite each other but we were having this conversation via messages. Rafsana, the Iranian student, I was sure it was her. That's what you get for being clever and trying to impress a pretty woman. I kicked myself, but I played dumb.

Could you be more specific? What did I say and to whom?

I can't say. A student mentioned to her tutor what you said and the tutor passed it on to Núria who passed it on to me.

Her tutor, she said, not his. So definitely Rafsana. Nasty, Iranian honey trapper. Why would she do that? What did she have to gain? But it was bad that it had got to Núria. She was married to one of the *illuminati*. Me and my big mouth. It was the crack about god and mammon, I was sure of it. But still I played dumb.

If I don't know what my crime is, how am I supposed to defend myself?

It's a difficult situation, she wrote back.

You could say that. Are you going to defend me?

I'll try.

I still have an email you sent where you say you don't know what you'd do without me.

That was about work.

I know it was. I didn't think it was a declaration of love. Did Núria tell you to get rid of me? Is that what you're going to do?

I'm not sure what I can do.

What I didn't say was: you could stand up for me as a valued member of staff. You could have a bit of backbone, show some loyalty. But you won't because you're shit scared. If I got kicked out, I could stop feeling bad about being such a hypocrite but my newly clear conscience wouldn't pay the rent or buy the children shoes. I was supping with the devil but I hadn't had my fill. I realise this made me as hypocritical as the rest of them, but needs must. Besides, when I leave I want it to be on my terms and by the front door. The time had come to use that leverage. I felt bad, because I didn't feel any malice towards Anna, but I didn't have any other weapon. I wrote:

Sagrera's wife is very religious, isn't she? Very old school. And she's a big pal of Núria's.

Everyone knows he's been arrested, she wrote back. It's all over the news.

Don't be cute, Anna. You know what I'm talking about.

No I don't and nor do you.

Yes, I do and you know I do. You know what this place is like. All the gossip, the whispering. No smoke without fire, that's what people will say. It will get back to your husband eventually, too.

Anna got up and left the room. She was even paler than usual when she came back and she looked like she'd been crying. Poor woman, her lover had been arrested and was quite possibly going to jail. And I was blackmailing her. It was like a country and western song. She had plenty to cry about. She sent me a message.

I'll speak to Núria. I'll see what I can do. I can't promise anything.

Thanks, I said. Much appreciated.

I got up to leave but she motioned me over. I stood behind her. She pointed at the headline.

I cried when I sacked 6,700 people.

It's what he said, Anna. You were there. He said it was the worst day of his life when he had to sack all those people, so bad that he cried.

I know. I know that's what he said.

So? I said, daring her to tell me what she didn't like about it, though I never imagined the headline would get past her.

Anna fixed me with her amber jade eyes. I had a pretty good idea what was coming next.

Me da miedo.

Motherland

It's only a matter of time before someone gets killed, said Isaac, naked but for a pair of shorts and beautiful in the way that the young are beautiful through the sheer fact and vitality of youth. He held a cold can of beer against his cheek.

Please be careful, Sonia said. I worry about you out there.

He gave her that look that said please don't make a fuss.

Don't worry, I'll be fine.

Will you? Someone will get killed, you said so yourself. What's to stop that someone being you?

Come on, I'm not stupid, mum, he said, as though stupidity had anything to do with it.

Isaac was right, of course; sooner or later someone would get killed. It was inevitable. What began with slogans and flag-waving had moved on to violence. If everyone continued to raise their game, as they had so far, someone would pay with their life, and that death would have to be avenged, and so it would go on.

Sonia looked across at the apartments opposite, mostly shuttered against the sun. The crushing heat had settled on the city for weeks, a life-sapping heat that dulled the senses and shortened tempers. The city was at war with itself. The riots, sporadic at first, were now almost routine. There were running battles. Rioters built barricades of plastic rubbish bins, then set them alight. The bitter stench of burning plastic replaced the city's peacetime aroma of piss and marijuana while the heat settled on its sleepless citizens like a fat, dirty hen, muting the sounds of life save for the summer soundtrack of surveillance helicopters clattering above the streets and the whoop-whoop of sirens.

Isaac had resisted the nationalist pull so far, with its easy answers to complex questions. Sonia admired him for that; it took guts, now that the tide was mostly running one way. He belonged to some sort of anarchist group which as far as she could tell took the position that it was all shit. Everything, whichever side they were on, which, given the general level of mendacity dressed up as righteous indignation, seemed like a legitimate position.

Later that afternoon, after Isaac had gone back out to do battle with whoever, Sonia's younger son Marc sat with his back to her as she pulled a nit comb gently through the boy's hair. She slid a bug from between the steel tines and crushed it between thumbnail and forefinger, then wiped the dark smear of blood on a cloth and watched as a helicopter hovering above their block banked away towards the north. The cat slept, stretched out in the shade, exhausted by the heat.

She drew the comb through Marc's damp, brown hair, wiped it on the cloth and inspected it for bugs and eggs. The boy, his skin honey brown, sat still and uncomplaining. Sonia repeated the procedure. The boy's hair was fine and straight and the comb didn't snag. She wiped the sweat from her brow with the back of her hand.

Find any? the boy asked.

A couple. Mostly eggs.

Black smoke rose beyond the roofline of the buildings opposite. Isaac was out there somewhere, face hidden behind a scarf, starting fires and running from the cops. The conflict had become like the weather, the oppressive heat; it just went on and on, no end in sight, nor apparently any will to end it. The worst sort of people had come to prominence and in turn brought out the worst in everyone else. Pandora's box was open. Now people shouted things that before they barely dared whisper, puffed up with righteous rage, salting their wounds, lest they heal, who was right and who was wronged, everyone but themselves to blame, insults at first, now stones and petrol bombs.

There were twelve apartments in the building. Seven of them sported nationalist flags tied to their balconies. Barely a month ago there were only five; a year ago just a couple. It frightened her, this consensus that was partly borne out of fear of standing out from the crowd. The word traitor circulated freely, often about anyone who refused to fall in line. She hated what was happening. It was as though everyone had lost their mind. She had lived here all her life but had begun to feel like a stranger in her own city.

Sonia wondered what she would do when her balcony was the last without a flag. Would she get one for the sake of a quiet life? Or would she say no, no flags for me? Would she make a principled stand?

Sonia looked up from grooming Marc. A plane came in low from the north, delivering another batch of tourists. They kept coming, despite the conflict, the riots and rubber bullets, the seemingly endless recession and the bogus economic recovery trumpeted by the government and the IMF but which had somehow failed to reach the people of all ages who slept in doorways and scrabbled in bins for food. Most visitors simply shut it out or didn't seem to notice; to others it was one more attraction. Sonia had seen tourists taking selfies with the riot squad baton-charging protesters as a backdrop.

She rested her hand for a moment on Marc's bare shoulder. The skin on the back of her hand was taking on a papery quality; another sign of age. It contrasted with Marc's smooth, flawless skin. She felt a surge of love for the boy as she crushed another bug with her nail. Her neighbours, except those whose balconies were still in the sun, sat out. Some read magazines, some fanned themselves, most just sat, waiting for the air to cool.

The sky clouded over and the pressure dropped. There was a vague sense of impending rain, but it was probably another false alarm. It was like the undertow of anticipation when the house lights dim and the orchestra starts tuning up, but then nothing happened, there was no concert. The rain never came.

Sonia's nearest neighbour was a woman in her late thirties with dyed red hair who was always reading. She sat on a blue folding chair, a book on her lap and a drink at her side on a small folding table. When they passed each other in the street or the market they exchanged smiles and said hello but never had a conversation. She had a round face and greenish eyes. The ice clinked in the glass as she put the drink to her lips and, sensing Sonia's gaze, caught her eye and raised the glass. Sonia held up the nit comb in salutation. The neighbour smiled faintly and went back to her book.

In the hotel opposite clients sat outside on the balconies even though they were still in full sun, the men shirtless, the women in bikinis or halter tops and shorts, their pale skin burnt pink and striped with strap marks. In the morning these transitory beings would be gone and the chambermaids – small, dark-skinned women in black uniforms and white aprons – would appear, sweeping balconies, cleaning the windows and stripping and making up the beds. It was as though the chambermaids were the rightful residents and the tourists, intruders who were permitted to stay a night or two, but whose existence was then swept away into a bin bag. On a hotel balcony a young woman in a skimpy dress sat on her boyfriend's knee. The boyfriend slid his hand between her thighs and she slapped it away playfully.

So they still do that, Sonia thought, girls still sit on their boyfriend's lap. It struck her as old fashioned, at once possessive and submissive. She imagined the couple were on holiday and would have sex later, if they hadn't already, and then go out for dinner.

I saw the world's biggest yacht this afternoon, Marc said. It's moored in the old port.

Really? What's it like?

It's huge. It's not like a yacht at all, it's a ship. As big as the ferry. Except it's a sort of yellow colour, not white like the others.

Do you know who owns it?

Some Russian guy. It cost €600 million. I Googled it. It's so big there's a bit where a helicopter can land. It's amazing.

Amazing, Sonia repeated.

What? Marc said, catching her tone.

Six hundred million. What a waste of money. Imagine how much good you could do with that much money.

Marc sighed. His mother had a way of raining on his parade. She could be a real downer at times.

It's just that I don't see why having masses of money and then showing off by spending it on a yacht is something to admire.

It's OK, mum, Marc said wearily. I get it.

Sonia felt bad. The kid was just making conversation and young boys like anything that's big; big is good, biggest is best. It didn't mean the boy approved of Russian oligarchs. She should have let it go. That was something people said about Sonia, that she was serious. It wasn't a compliment; it was a complaint.

I'm sorry, she said. I didn't mean to go on.

The boy shrugged. She continued combing, although she'd probably got all the nits and eggs by now, but she wanted to hold on to the moment, a peaceful, human animal moment, primeval, the way apes groom one another, and the tender love she felt for the child. Marc was an easy-going boy. He abhorred conflict, unlike his older brother who was born feeling short-changed, always indignant, as though the life he'd been given wasn't the one advertised in the brochure. Marc, on the other hand, was like a balm to Sonia's chafed soul.

She found it hard to let things go (that was another complaint). She was forever questioning, interrogating. Even this peaceful moment with Marc, she couldn't just accept that she felt at peace, happy even, in spite of everything. No, she held the feeling of peace up to the light and examined it, rather than let it simply lap against her inner shoreline. And the act of examination changed it; it always did. However clear and unalloyed the sentiment, once examined it became suffused with melancholy, like a splash of Angostura bitters clouding a glass of gin.

Are we done? Marc asked. I have to go soon.

Yeah, we're done. Bug free, for now at least.

She set the comb and cloth down on the table. Marc leaned his smooth brown back against his mother and rested his head against her. Sonia caressed his shoulder absent-mindedly.

Marc was going to spend the weekend with a friend who lived a few blocks away. Then next weekend the friend would come to stay. That way each set of parents got a weekend without children. Sonia looked forward to her child-free time, but as soon as Marc went she always felt bereft. There was Isaac, of course, but he came and went as he pleased, passing through the fridge like a one-man plague of locusts before heading back out or retreating to his bedroom. Marc was ten and Isaac nineteen. Half her life had been set to their rhythm.

Two boys, two fathers, two separations. Not a brilliant track record, she'd be the first to admit. Isaac's father left her for another man. She didn't see that coming. With Marc's father it was less dramatic. After Marc was born, he seemed to lose interest in life and in her. They ate in silence, they never went anywhere together, they stopped having sex. She asked him to leave and he left.

Have you got your stuff ready?

Yup.

OK, give us a kiss and off you go. See you Sunday.

She held him against her, steeping herself in his aroma of young, sunned skin. Marc wriggled out of her embrace and was gone with a bang of the door. The cat pricked up one ear but didn't move. For the first half hour after he left she felt unmoored and momentarily at sea. Of late she'd felt increasingly – what was it? – redundant. As a mother, that is. Not that a mother was all she was but it had become her core. Everything else was what she did; being a mother was what she was.

She thought about Isaac, so cocksure and carefree. Young men crave action, that was part of it. Women bring life, men bring death, that was Sonia's sister's take. That was a bit extreme, but her sister had a point. Making and nurturing life is a drawn out, laborious and often tedious enterprise. Nurture is by its very nature repetitive, a slow grind producing even slower progress. It is not glamorous. There are no computer games where the object is to soothe a wailing child or where the player gets points for not losing their cool when a senile parent asks the same question for the tenth time in as many minutes.

So hard to make a life, so easy to take it, she thought. But nurture can't compete with murder; murder has all the panache that nurture lacks. Hands on hips, it's chic and sleek. It speaks a snappy vernacular: waste, smoke, blow away, chill, clip, top, whack. Murder has finesse, verve, élan. In contrast, nurture mumbles and shambles, dishevelled, one of its buttons is undone, there is a damp stain on its shoulder. Nurture's vocabulary is just as limp: nurse, nourish, foster, sustain. Ending a life takes a moment and has all the brio of decisive action. These are virtues of the moment, they cannot be sustained, a life cannot be lived with finesse; life is too long for that. A life is made and re-made; it doesn't make such good theatre as death. Death can be delivered in style - the blunt beauty of the small automatic, the spangle of light on the blade before it plunges into the dark organ, the kung fu kick, the karate chop, the uppercut that lifts you off your feet and out of this world – a single act that puts an end to all others. It's well documented that men are often sexually aroused by the act of killing. Sonia didn't know what to make of that; that the act of ending a life should stimulate a man's life-making apparatus.

The neighbour across the way looked up at the sky and untied her flag from the balcony. Sonia laughed. Even if it did rain, the flags were made of polyester.

The neighbour caught her eye as she folded the flag and raised her left hand in the nationalist salute. Sonia didn't return the salute.

A helicopter held a position about five blocks north. An ambulance passed. Sonia knew the difference between one siren and another. She thought about Isaac, and almost immediately shut out the thought. There was no reason to think the ambulance was for him. The redhead across the way refreshed her glass and settled back into her book.

As the sun went off the balconies, more neighbours appeared. The young man on the hotel balcony slid his girlfriend off his knee and went inside. He reappeared with two cans of beer. Sonia looked at her phone. Riots had broken out at various points in the city. The nationalist leader defended people's right to protest at the interior minister's visit. It was, in effect, a call to arms. The leader of the opposition, afraid of being on the wrong side of history, made a lame appeal for calm. All police leave had been cancelled.

A sudden escalation in the violence, according to a police spokesman. There were reports of a fatality during clashes on the airport road. There are no other details at present, the spokesman said. Please don't let it be Isaac, Sonia said out loud. She looked up at the sky.

I wish it would rain, she said.

Sonia watched the news stream on her phone. A reporter gave a to-camera piece from the scene of the riot. The reporter looked anxious as people milled around him, pulling faces and shaking their fists. Sonia searched for Isaac in the crowd. The reporter said a large crowd ambushed the interior minister's car on its way from the airport. Police baton charged the crowd and fired rubber bullets. There were conflicting accounts about what had happened. Protesters claimed the victim died as a result of police brutality; the police said he was hit on the head after rioters started hurling paving stones. The fatality, as the reporter insisted on calling the dead man, had been identified but police were not releasing his name until his family had been informed. He was thought to be 19 years old.

Jesus, no, please no.

The reporter read out a statement from the president saying he deeply regretted the loss of life and his thoughts and prayers were with the family of the deceased.

Fuck you, Sonia said to the screen. You started this; this is on you.

She sent Isaac another message. Please call me.

The helicopter was back. On the hotel balcony opposite the woman who had been sitting on her boyfriend's knee had dressed up for the evening and was taking selfies. On the next balcony, two young women, white as milk, with sunburned chests and shoulders, were drinking cava from plastic cups. The humidity was so high the air seemed to press against her flesh. Once again there was a sense of an impending storm, a glowering sky off to the northwest. Maybe this time it was more than a rehearsal, maybe this time it would really rain.

She tried not to think about Isaac but the thought wouldn't go away. The victim was nineteen, that's all she knew. He said someone's going to get killed and she said what's to stop that someone being you. She wished she'd never said that. It felt like a curse, like asking for bad luck.

There was thunder, it was definitely thunder, though distant. The red-haired neighbour was out, book on her lap, drink at hand. Sonia wanted a drink herself but resisted, feeling she needed her head to be clear, in case. She didn't linger on in case of what.

The thunder rolled, though still far away, and the temperature began to drop. The cat sat up, eyes wide and fur fluffed up, ears turned like scanners towards the northwest, where the weather was coming from. The sunbathing women shivered and retreated indoors. Most of the tourists had gone inside – they hadn't come all this way for a thunderstorm – while the neighbours began gathering on their balconies, thirsty for rain, or at least a break in the weather. For half an hour the thunder rumbled on without getting any closer. The helicopter went away, retreating from the impending storm.

The temperature had dropped sharply and the sky darkened to a murky blue-black. A chill wind picked up. The screeching swifts disappeared. The cat's fur stood on end and its ears twitched like antennae The baby in the apartment below, a child that cried almost without pause, fell silent. Sonia shivered. Shivering was a pleasant and all but forgotten sensation. The thunder rumbled on and sheet lightning lit the sky. But there was still no rain. It continued like that for another half hour; the cracks of thunder closer and louder and the lightning stark against the darkening sky. Sonia sat and shivered. There was no news, or just the same news on a loop. She wished her boys were home, altogether, safe from harm, wagons in a circle.

A solitary fat drop of rain landed splat on the terrace below. Everyone looked up to see if there was more to come. There was another drop - splat - then another and another – splat, splat, splat - then the rain was plop-plopping in fat drops but it still felt like a tease, these few drops, it wasn't real rain, not the downpour that had been promised all day.

And then it came. The thunder cracked right above their heads and the cat fled indoors. The rain came down as though someone had kicked open a sluice, a deluge, a tumultuous curtain of water, improbable as Hollywood rain, accompanied by thunder cracks as the lightning fizzed across the sky, like the grand finale of a bombastic stadium rock concert. The rain fell so hard and thick that Sonia could barely see across to the hotel where a few guests stood, still in their shorts, pale arms folded, disconsolate. Everyone else was out now, just watching it rain. It was spectacular.

Sonia sensed someone behind her and turned to see Isaac in the doorway. In a second she passed through oh thank god, you're safe, to why the fuck didn't you answer my messages but before she could speak she was silenced by the look of distress on his face. He was nineteen years old with a stubbly beard but what she saw was a frightened little boy in need of comfort.

She put her arms around him and held him tightly, claiming him, fastening him to her. He smelled of sweat and hormones. He didn't pull away like he usually did, but let his arms flop loosely around her shoulders, acquiescing to her embrace, but reluctant at first to return it. He was taller than her. His chin rested on her shoulder, cheek to cheek. His body was hard and spare. She could feel him needing to cry, knowing he wouldn't. They stood like that for a minute or two, taking comfort from each other.

Do you want to talk about it?

He shook his head against hers.

Did you know the boy who died? Was he a friend of yours?

Sort of, not really. I knew him from, you know, around.

What happened?

It was crazy. Everyone just sort of lost it. Totally. He got beaten up really badly. I saw it. There was nothing I could do.

By the cops?

No, it wasn't the cops.

So here we go, Sonia thought. A martyr to the cause, though she didn't know which cause. It probably didn't matter.

Isaac disentangled himself and they turned to watch the downpour. He stood behind his mother, resting his hands on her shoulders, her little boy, now a head taller than her. She leaned her head against his chest just as earlier Marc had leaned his against her. The red-headed neighbour stood at the railing of her balcony, out of the shelter of the balcony above, soaked to the skin, hair plastered to her head, with her arms aloft, like a diva in a tragic opera about to deliver an aria. She turned to Sonia and started laughing, a joyous, crazy laugh as the rain sluiced off the roofs and sheeted down from the overflowing gutters and for the first time in weeks the air smelled fresh and clean and new.

You're crying, mum.

Sonia sniffed and nodded.

Why?

Why? Did there have to be a why? Because it was raining at last and the rain at least was something tangible, something real and unvitiated amid all the posturing, all the bad blood and manufactured hatred and flags and declarations and pettiness and above all the ceaseless, relentless, life-sapping mendacity of it all. And because her son was here with her and he was young and alive and beautiful simply by existing and she loved him beyond reason because having children meant that come what may you were condemned to be desperately, terrifyingly, irrevocably in love with them for the rest of your days and because it was someone else's boy who died, someone else's loss, not hers, and right now the rain was washing everything away, the heat, the hypocrisy, the hatred and it felt like they'd waited forever for this and just then she could imagine this was the beginning of something new, something better. Sonia reached up and took both his hands in hers.

It's nothing, sweetheart, she said. I'm just crying, that's all.

Epiphany

It's about being in the moment, Daniela said. You have to imagine that you exist beyond what you're thinking. Think of it as nowness.

Nowness, Gabriel said aloud, to himself and to the Atlantic at his feet, putting the word out there, hoping the word itself might anchor him for a moment, in the moment. Nowness: it was succinct, a trifle ugly, perhaps, but then he tended to be a bit precious about language. There was no mistaking its meaning, nor what Daniela was trying to tell him - nowness was not his forte.

He had brought himself to Finisterre, the end of the earth, because he needed to think. This was typical; he could just as well have done his thinking in the park or in a café, but he imagined that this physical displacement might also provoke a shift in his inner topography. And so he'd come to this wild place at the edge of the world, the vast Atlantic so seductively calm and benignly blue it seemed you could just push out in a little makeshift boat and be in the New World in time for lunch. He thought of all the small boats and the thousands who had set sail from these coasts, pursuing a dream with heavy hearts and empty pockets, the drowned and the saved.

There you go again, he said, still thinking aloud. This is what Daniela means. Here you are telling stories instead of being in the moment, just being here with nothing but the sea and sky with its great whisks and rents of cloud. It reminded him of Connemara, that same edge of the world sensation. The comparison was yet one more manifestation of a failure to focus, of his restless, flitting dragonfly of a life, a life illuminated – he liked to believe - by an occasional iridescent flash of brilliance. As if that made up for all the darting and dithering.

I feel like I'm on the cusp of something, he said. This was a week ago. They were in the kitchen, him leaning against the door jamb with a glass of something white, Daniela at the worktop, making kofte.

Daniela's only response was a sidelong flick of the eye. She took a blob of the spiced lamb and pine nuts mixture, rolled it between her palms into a cigar-shaped log and dropped it on to a plate. Lately she'd been talking about mindfulness. We live in a world of distraction, she said. We're losing the ability to focus. I'm trying to teach myself to be in the moment, to concentrate on one thing at a time instead of doing three things at once.

Usually, she put music on when she was cooking, or sometimes the radio, but not today. Gabriel wondered if that was part of being in the moment, making kofte without distractions. Mindfully.

Daniela rolled another kofte. I wouldn't mind a glass of that, she said. He peeled himself from the jamb and took the wine from the fridge.

This mindfulness thing isn't some big deal, she continued, choosing not to pursue what he'd said about being on the cusp of whatever. She knew he'd get there in his own time. It's not a philosophy. A lot of it is just about not looking at your phone every five seconds. You see people on the metro, nearly every single one is looking at a screen. Connected, but connected to what? Not to where they are, to their surroundings or other people.

You know when you've got something on the tip of your tongue, he said, handing her the glass of wine. She took it in her greasy fingers and raised it and her eyebrows in salute. It was as if they were speaking in parallel, disconnected, like a David Mamet script.

A word or a name you can't quite reach, he said. Or when you wake from a dream and you're left with the feel of it, but not the content. It's like that. I feel like I'm on the threshold but I don't know of what.

He felt a surge of fondness for her as she rolled the meat between her pinkening palms. A wayward ringlet unpinned itself but she couldn't put it back with her greasy hands. He pinned it back under a hair grip. Gabriel waited, a little anxiously, for her response. Daniela could be as blunt as she was sharp. It was part of her attraction, but her words sometimes stung.

I assume this is about writing, Gabriel, this cusp?

He sipped the wine and said yes with his eyes.

But I don't know what it is. A way of saying, a new and a different way of saying. Maybe. I feel I need to walk it around, see what comes. Walking works.

You can walk around here.

True. But I think a change of scene might trigger something.

Daniela was supportive of his writing, he had no complaints on that score, but he felt it was also something she only tolerated, like living with an obsessive. One time when someone asked, how's Gabriel, he overheard her say, oh, you know, off somewhere playing with his imaginary friends. He was pretty sure she knew he could hear.

Another time, when they were having dinner, Daniela said, à propos of nothing in particular: you've been sleeping with one of your characters, haven't you? That sex scene in the chapter you showed me, I know that woman, she runs that new bar, the one with the blue tiles and the awful music. It's her, isn't it?

It's not exactly a sex scene.

OK, it's an as yet unconsummated sex scene. But I'm right, aren't I? It's her.

Not really.

Based on her, then. She's your model. You like her, don't you?

Gabriel shrugged.

Don't you think it's a bit weird the way you put women you fancy in your books so you can sleep with them by proxy?

Weird?

Yes, weird. Sort of voyeuristic. Or like you're stalking them.

Would you rather I slept with them in real life?

No, but I'd rather you spent less time fantasising about other women, but I guess that's what men do, always on the prowl, even if it's just in your imagination. That said, I think the scene is really well written, very convincing.

So what happens next? Does he sleep with her?

I'm not sure. She's married. Her husband's a cop. It's tricky.

A dangerous liaison, then. I look forward to it.

The wine glass was smeared with her fingerprints. She rolled another kofte. They'd been together for 12 years. Long enough to take the edge off some things. But it also meant most of the corners had been rounded off, even with Daniela, who had some pretty sharp angles. Gabriel loved her. It was a soft, not a fierce love, like reaching a clearing after a long haul in the woods, a pool of light. People found her difficult, uncompromising, not afraid to speak her mind. He could see why but paradoxically he found in her a source of calm. Gabriel wondered if it was this tranquillity that he wanted to disrupt, if that was what the cusp was about, that he was afraid of tranquillity or mistook it for tedium.

I'm thinking I might go away for a few days, he said. Try to get a handle on this.

The kofte was made. She laid them out on an oiled baking tray, like rows of corpses.

Our very own Srebrenica, he said.

Daniela rolled her eyes. You always have to take everything up a notch, don't you? I'm not sure you're a great candidate for mindfulness, she said, sliding the tray under the grill. It wasn't that she was ignoring what he said about going away, but once she had a thought, she liked to see it through before moving on to the next thing. She was very linear.

I'm just restless by nature.

No, Gabriel, mi amor, you're not just restless. Restless

barely covers it at all. You're a fugitive. I can't really see how you could learn to live in the moment when you're always running ahead of yourself, she said, wiping her hands on her apron. You're always thinking how the moment, any moment, can be recycled into something else. It's not an accusation; it's what you do. Reality for you is a sort of dry run for fiction. Life is the raw material, fiction the product, the added value. Frankly, I doubt that you know which is which anymore. But in any case, if you think you need to be somewhere else to get a hold of this thing, off you go. Did you have somewhere in mind?

Well, I thought of doing the Camino de Santiago. I've wanted to do it for years.

Daniela gave him a look.

It's OK, I'm not going to do it. It takes 30 days to do the whole thing from Saint Jean Pied de Port to Santiago de Compostela.

Thirty days is too long.

Daniela said whenever he went away she looked forward to the solitude and then within a day was wishing he'd come back. He felt the same; he pictured himself as a loner but loneliness always got the better of him. He was much more of a homebody than he cared to admit.

I thought of doing a stretch, maybe Pamplona to Burgos, but even that's 10 days.

In the end, as though working through a lengthy mathematical calculation to which the answer is ultimately zero, he flew directly to Santiago.

His flight was delayed and as his irritation rose he

thought about what Daniela said and tried to stay in the moment. He told himself that nothing he did would make the plane get there any sooner. He should stay calm, focus on being where he was. There was no hurry, after all. He tried but it didn't work. It was an airport; airports are for departures and arrivals, not for being. They are not conducive to serenity.

Later he tried to stay in the moment when they were all on the plane and then missed their slot because a passenger whose bags were already stowed had dallied in the bar and hadn't boarded. He tried again while the crew went through the safety routine which no one listens to because everyone knows that, in the event of landing on water, as the crew put it, everyone will start screaming and inflate their life jackets while still on the plane and get stuck in the emergency exits and they'll all be trampled to death before they even get a chance to drown.

He tried not to think ahead, not to wish himself anywhere but where he was. But soon he was itching for them to take off and then, once airborne, anxious to arrive as soon as possible. He willed the trolley to move a little faster down the aisle so he could ask for a beer. Do I really want a beer, he asked himself? No, not really, but when the trolley appeared alongside, his lips dutifully shaped themselves into the words, a beer, please.

People say the journey's the thing, but flying is merely transition, not travel as such; a lacuna between departure and arrival, not an experience in itself. The moment the flight began, he longed for it to end. As Daniela said, he wasn't a great candidate for mindfulness. As the plane taxied to the terminal he reached for his mobile to switch it back on but then thought better of it. We have to stop looking at our phones every five seconds, Daniela said. Fine, he wouldn't look at it at all.

He arrived on a warm, bright day under a vast, blue-white sky. Santiago itself had a northern feel; the architecture veered between Stoic practicality and bourgeois elegance. After he'd booked into a hotel he wandered around and soon found himself in the huge Plaza Obradoiro, dominated by the basilica that was the pilgrims' final destination. The cathedral façade was an impressive example of fear-of-god baroque, but the interior, was vulgar, gilded kitsch.

The penitents and pilgrims queued to kiss the hem of the garment of the small effigy of Santiago. The confession boxes that lined one side of the nave were, unusually for modern Spain, actually occupied by priests hearing confession. He promised Daniela he'd light a candle for her sister who died of cancer. It was something they did from time to time, and always on the day of the dead; a soothing, ancient ritual that secular society fails to offer, the solitary flame in a quiet place of reflection.

In the basilica, however, there were no candles. Instead, there was a board with a grid of tiny light bulbs, basically white fairy lights. You put a euro in the slot and a bulb lit up for a day. This really wasn't the same as lighting a candle; it was dull and mechanical and lacked all the ritual of buying the candle from a whey-faced cleric then lighting it with a broken wick at the feet of your chosen saint or martyr. A light bulb emits a dim, constant light. You can't gaze upon it the way you can a flickering candle and reflect on life's evanescence. As a Catholic, Gabriel was shocked. If there's one thing the Church does well, it's death. Death is its strong suit. Just as well I didn't spend a month walking here, Gabriel thought, if a bunch of fairy lights is the best they can offer a weary pilgrim.

Later, he lay on the hotel bed and studied the map of Galicia and set his heart on Finisterre. To get there he had to take the road along the Costa da Morte, the coast of death. So now he had a plan: drive up the coast of death to the end of the earth, an itinerary perfectly suited to his romantic and melodramatic sensibility.

The following morning, he drove north, the Atlantic coast road punctuated by battered villages where he scarcely saw a child or a woman of childbearing age; nearly all the inhabitants appeared to be over sixty-five, many of them bent, elderly women in pinafores and gumboots and broad-brimmed straw hats.

There were roadworks north of Muros. He passed a sign apologising for the inconvenience caused by works designed to improve access to the coast of death. That raised a smile. The radio was playing Wild Horses by the Stones, or los Rolling as the DJ called them. The song flashed him back to his first true love, Sinéad, back home in Dublin. They were sixteen and spent one blissful year together, ecstatically in love, discovering sex and alcohol and marijuana. "Wild horses, we'll ride them some day." As it turned out, she rode away from Gabriel in a Ford Mondeo. She left him for a man of twenty who had his own car. Gabriel was heartbroken but he knew he couldn't compete.

They met again years later in London and were friends for a while. She was already drinking heavily by then, mostly whisky and ginger ale. She was a maudlin drunk. In her cups she told Gabriel, repeatedly, that he was the only good man she'd ever been with. She even apologised for dumping him for Mondeo man all those years ago. Now and then she'd call up drunk and he let her talk, knowing she wouldn't remember a word of it the next day. Then she stopped calling.

Years later he wondered what had become of her. He Googled her and all he found was a death notice in a south London newspaper. He tracked her daughter down to an address in Battersea. She said her mother died in a house fire. She had a favourite chair, her drinking chair, and passed out with a cigarette in her hand and set the house alight.

This is what you get for driving up the coast of death, he said to himself, memories like that. But he remembered her like it was yesterday, lying naked in his single bed, the two of them smoking Sweet Aftons, listening to the Stones, giddy with astonishment at what could be achieved with hands and lips and skin and absolutely no money whatsoever. The unrepeatable glory of first love.

The road to Finisterre was dotted with pilgrims, scallop shells tied to their backpacks, decked out in boots and the oversize walking stick that marked them out from regular walkers. Evidently walking to Santiago wasn't sufficient penance for some sinners who needed to go that extra mile.

There he was by the Finisterre lighthouse, at the edge of the world, looking out to sea, hoping for enlightenment. How many times had he done this? The wind in his hair, squinting into the bright marine light, the open sea – the Atlantic, Pacific, Mediterranean, Aegean, the Tasman - waiting for revelation, poised for that sunburst moment of clarity, the epiphany that never quite comes but instead dissolves into a vague sense of melancholy, followed by a hankering for a gin and tonic, or sex, sometimes both. He got to his feet, brushed the dust from his trousers and, for want of a revelation, headed back to the hire car.

Gabriel didn't much like the look of the town of Finisterre itself. It was a pinched and struggling place that seemed to want to live up to its name. He headed back down the coast and stopped at Carnota, a granite seaside village. He booked into a pensión that was little more than a bar with a few tables and a couple of rooms to let.

He left his bag in his room and went for a stroll. The entire village was hewn from granite, the houses, the pavement, the benches - all of it. There wasn't much to look at so he walked down the sea. He sat on a sand dune and watched the sunset and the light fade as the sea turned from blue-black to deep purple. He thought of phoning Daniela, just to say hi, I'm here. But if he turned his phone on there would be messages and after that he'd start reading the news and then he'd go on to social media and there would be no end to it.

Before mobiles no one expected you to check in every five minutes. Now people on planes texted, we're taking off, and then when they got there, we've landed. He did it himself. It was silly. He wondered how anyone got away with having an affair these days. You could never say you couldn't find a phone or the only pay phone had been vandalized. These days you couldn't even claim there was no mobile cover. He saw people on their mobiles in Finisterre, so if there was cover at the end of the earth there must be cover everywhere. He even knew couples who used a geo-locating app so they could see where their other half was at any given moment. Gabriel thought that was creepy, even if you don't have anything to hide. Daniela said a friend discovered her husband was having an affair because when she looked up an address on StreetView there he was in a bar at an outside table with a woman she'd never seen before. They were sitting too close together for it to have been business, she said.

He adored Daniela, even if sometimes he had to get away from her to see just how much he adored her. There was a word for it, uxorious: having or showing a great or excessive fondness for one's wife, according to the Oxford English Dictionary. Why excessive? Who set the limit on acceptable fondness? He savoured the word, uxorious. English was so rich and yet what was the point of using a word like uxorious if hardly anyone knew what it meant. People would say he was pretentious or showing off.

He worried about Daniela. She wasn't nearly as tough as she made out. What people saw and what put a lot of people off, that sharp tongue and quiet ferocity, was self-protection, a No Trespassing sign to stop people blundering into her fragile hinterland. She was like a cat with its fur standing on end, trying to look bigger and fiercer than it really is. But she trusted Gabriel, she let him in. She gave him a backstage pass to her heart. He was allowed to see her, unmasked and without make-up, on the understanding that what he saw there was classified information and not for sharing with the wider world. Uxorious; he wondered if there was a word that meant a great or excessive fondness for one's husband. He suspected not, as the fawning adoration of a husband was considered the norm.

It was nearly dark when he returned to the village. He dined on octopus and salad and greenish white wine. He was in a good mood when he got back to the bar where he was staying. Two elderly men were playing cards at a corner table. The TV above the bar was on with no sound. Gabriel took a seat at the bar and ordered a cognac.

Here on holiday? the bar owner asked. Gabriel shook his head.

I'm working, kind of.

What work do you do?

I'm a writer.

In his head it always sounded like, I'm a wanker. In other people's heads, too, he imagined, though not in Spanish at least.

Would I have heard of you? he asked.

People always ask that. What they mean is, are you famous? Not are you any good or what is it you're trying to say? What they mean is, will people make fun of me because I didn't ask for a selfie with you? How famous would you have to be for a barman in a village near Finisterre to have heard of you? Stephen King? Tolkien? Though who knows, maybe the man was a keen reader.

Maybe. One of my novels has been translated into numerous languages, including Spanish. He told the barman the title.

If the barman was impressed it didn't show. Gabriel could have said: After the success of my novel, City of Dreams, I was tipped as one of Ireland's most promising young writers. One to look out for, a reviewer wrote. Except Gabriel was no longer young and, if sales were the yardstick, he'd failed to live up to his promise. His three subsequent books were, in the industry parlance, well received, meaning a few decent reviews but poor sales. His sixth had only recently been published, so it was early days. His agent said, I have a good feeling about this one, Gabriel, I really do. But he always said that, forever hoping that his goose might squeeze out one more golden egg.

So you've come here to write? He refilled Gabriel's nearly empty glass

I need some peace and quiet. Some space. This seemed like a good bet.

You'll get plenty of that here. Quiet as the grave and sometimes just as cold.

The next morning he was up early. The beach at Carnota was completely undeveloped: there were no hotels, no buildings at all, and at seven kilometres from end to end it would take Gabriel most of the day to walk to the end and back again. It was perfect. The beach curved wide and flat between two headlands and the vastness of it all – ocean, sky, the dunes and flatlands behind the beach – produced a sensation of being at the bottom of the world. He walked barefoot on the hard, wet sand at the edge of the water. In the far distance someone was throwing a stick for a dog but he was otherwise alone. He walked all morning, not thinking about anything in particular, no nearer to discovering what he thought he was on the cusp of. He succumbed to nostalgia, a sweet melancholy tugging at the heart, not sad; more hankering than handkerchief.

At the northern end of the beach there was an outcrop of yellow rock beside the mouth of a small river. He climbed the rock and watched the waves break below. People who want to write a novel get the notion that they must rent a house by the sea in order to write it, even though what the sea inspires most are daydreams and wistfulness and the melancholy he felt earlier, not the requisite bum-in-chair time that creation demands. The rhythmic shush of the breaking waves, the push and pull of the tides, supply the perfect backdrop for a profound meditation on nothing in particular.

He'd been there maybe an hour, lulled into empty-headedness by the unaccustomed tranquillity, when a school of dolphins passed, seven of them, looping across the bay, about a hundred metres out to sea. He reached for the words to describe them then stopped and said to himself, no, don't say it, don't say anything. It was then that he knew an epiphany of sorts was at hand.

Daniela's words came back to him, about reality being just a dry run for fiction. It was all narrative, a narrative that he was already writing before the story had even begun to unfold. His story, other people's stories, the dolphins.

In a flash he saw that all along, words – his beloved words - had served him as a kind of armour, that striving to say a thing well only obscured the thing not said, the thing he was afraid to or didn't know how to say. Some people hide behind silence, for fear of ending up on their own confessional talk show. Gabriel hid behind words. Could this really be true, he asked himself? That, while ostensibly pursuing the *mot juste*, he actually used the imprecision of words in order to shelter in their ambiguity? Had he used words merely as a defence, a shield, a means of pinning life down, to quell the chaos, to shape life but also to keep it at arm's length? What did it mean, this epiphany? That now it was time to write for real, to really write? On the contrary, it was clear - horrifyingly so - that the logic of what he was thinking was that he should stop, that he shouldn't write at all. It wasn't about finding a new way with words, the time had come to shut up and say nothing, to cast off the narrative disguise and cease to darken the plain page with words.

He had lived too much outside himself, an observer, taking notes, scripting his own drama, telling the story, hurrying ahead but always that little bit behind, like a movie soundtrack that is out of sync. He lived his life as a starting point for a story about what came next. But this, the here and now, right now this moment, was what came next. It was so clear. He sat on the yellow rock where the river trickled into the sea. The air was fresh and cool. A bank of dirty white cloud hung across the horizon like a furled sail. There you go, that's your trouble right there, he said out loud. Metaphor. That word, like. It's a cloud; why does it have to be like something else, why can't it just be a cloud? All those thoughts and phrases that begin, it was like, it was as if, it was as though – each of them a harbinger of an incoming metaphor. It was unnecessary; it didn't add to the sum of anything, didn't make the cloud more interesting. It didn't make it more knowable.

As these thoughts crystallised he felt a huge sense of relief, unchained, liberated. Things would be different from now on; he would stop the narrative. It was a time to be, not to tell. He would stop looking for the right word and look for the thing itself, and stop fretting if the book he was writing was as good as the last, if the next one would be better, if he'd ever write another as good as City of Dreams. Instead, he could turn his back on the whole business, just walk away, no more books. He wouldn't write anything, not another word. He felt elated, like he'd just kicked a bad habit. Then almost immediately the anxiety set in: if he didn't write, what would he do? More to the point, who would he be? When, years ago, he finally quit smoking, a habit he'd had so long it was totally enmeshed in his sense of self, his greatest concern was could he still be himself without cigarettes? Would people accept him, would they like him as much? Or would they say, oh right, Gabriel, I knew him back when he smoked; that was the real Gabriel. It was absurd but the anxiety was there. Of course, he could still be himself without tobacco, but writing was another matter; without writing, who would he be?

Daniela said that the thing about nowness was that you can start to see things in a different way, from a different angle. And when that happens, she said, you should just sit with it. Let it be. Let it settle. So that's what he did, he sat with it on the beach at Carnota, and tried not to think, not to fret about what life would be like after this, what he would be like. He tried not to look ahead, anticipate. He said aloud: I said to my soul be still, and let the silence come upon you. That was Eliot, one of the Quartets, he couldn't remember which. He could Google it, but he said to himself, be still, you don't need to Google it. It doesn't matter.

The temperature dropped suddenly and the sky darkened. The dirty white cloud on the horizon that looked like a furled sail wasn't a metaphor; it was a weather front and it was no longer on the horizon. In the space of a few moments the sky went from blue to grey to black. The thunder rolled and the first fat drop of rain slapped on to the stone beside him. The rain was falling heavily by the time he got down from the rocks but he was still five hundred metres from the thin shelter of the trees. Within a minute he was soaked, and a minute later so wet his feet squelched in his shoes. He laughed out loud; there was nothing else to do but laugh. By the time he made it to the trees, which in any case were little more than bushes, the worst of the storm had passed, sweeping over the granite village to the hills beyond. The rain dripped down his face and neck, it trickled down his back and into his sodden shoes. He laughed again at the melodrama of it all; first the epiphany and then this drenching like a baptism, a rebirth.

He took out his mobile and switched it on. He felt an urgent need to tell Daniela about his epiphany, how everything was going to be different from now on. Despite the soaking, the phone appeared to be working. There were several messages, dozens of them, in fact, some from Daniela and half a dozen from Seb, his agent. He didn't open them but instead called Daniela.

Daniela, it's me, I just called...

Oh, Gabriel, I was just thinking about you. How are you?

Soaking wet, as it happens. There was a huge storm but it's passed now. But never mind, I feel like, I don't know, something just happened, I feel like I just woke up.

I'm not surprised. It's been a long wait. You must be so chuffed.

Chuffed? Well, not really. Confused, more than anything. You know I said I felt like I was on the cusp of something? Well, it's not quite what I imagined, a big change, in fact, really big. I've realised, I've decided ...

And then he lost the connection. Emergency cover only, the screen said. Jesus, he'd just had a revelation, an epiphany. Doesn't that count as an emergency? And why did she say he must be chuffed? At what? It didn't make sense. Something must have happened. Maybe that was what all the messages were about. But before he could check them his mobile rang.

Hi, what I was starting to say, Daniela, is, I mean, suddenly it was so clear, that I don't need to ...

Hello, is this Gabriel Devlin's mobile?

It wasn't Daniela's voice. It was a well-spoken young English woman with the clear diction and slightly sibilant "S" acquired in England's better schools and elite universities. He paused for a moment.

Yes, this is me, he said, a little uncertainly, as though he were no longer sure.

Oh excellent, she said with an enthusiasm that he didn't feel the information merited. My name is Emma Devereux (she pronounced it Devro). I'm calling from the BBC in London.

The words and the accent conjured an image of scratchy black and white footage, a man in evening dress with pomaded hair solemnly speaking cut-glass English into an enormous microphone: This is the BBC in London.

Hello, Emma. I'm sorry, I thought you were someone else. What can I do for you?

I'm calling from The Book Program. Are you familiar with it?

Yes, of course.

Oh good. We were hoping you would agree to be one of our guests on next week's program. It would be great if you could make it. Oh, and congratulations, by the way.

Congratulations?

Yes, for the Mann Booker?

The Booker? I'm sorry, I've been off the grid for a while. Disconnected.

Oh my god. You mean you don't know? You've been long-listed.

Long-listed? Really? For the Booker?

Yes, for The Road to Somewhere. That's why we'd like you to join us, if you can.

Gabriel stood by a granite barn, the rain dripping off his hair and along his fingers and down the back of the hand that held the phone. The Booker long list; he'd never got this close before. Even City of Dreams only picked up a minor award. He felt almost sick with excitement. He didn't know what to say, or what to think.

Hello, are you still there?

Hello, yes. Sorry. You've sort of taken me by surprise.

A pleasant surprise though, I imagine.

Oh, yes. Oh god, yes.

His voice caught and for a moment he thought he was about to burst into tears.

Super. Well, I'll let you catch your breath. Meanwhile, if it's all right with you, we'll send you a formal invitation and some notes on the format. We'd be delighted if you agree to appear. I'm sure our listeners will be dying to hear more about the book.

Yes, of course. I'd be happy to. What I mean is, I'll have to think about it, he added, aware that he was babbling like a child. May I ask who else will be on the program?

She told him. One was a personal bête noire, a critic who wrote a review of his third novel in the Observer in which he commented that Devlin is one of those frustrating authors who sails close to greatness but, the moment it hoves into sight, changes tack and runs aground in the shallows. Snide, pompous bastard, Gabriel said when he read it.

I'll have to check with my agent, but in principle I'd be delighted. Thank you for inviting me.

Not at all. I'll be in touch. Bye for now.

His heart was racing and his hands were shaking. Only minutes ago he was walking away from writing, from the whole neurosis of it, the trying to find words for things that could otherwise just be let be, and then fretting that they weren't the right words anyway, there were other, better words; there were always better words. He had a vision of liberation, a whole new life was opening up before him, a life without imaginary friends. And now this, a glimpse of glory after all these years. His head was spinning. Ok, it was only the long list, but that alone could be a huge boost to sales, and then if he made it on to the short list. He pictured himself accepting the award. Ladies and gentlemen of the jury, I feel at once thrilled and humbled. Oh, stop it, he told himself. He should call his agent; that was the next step. Then his mobile rang.

It was Daniela. He let it ring a couple of times, then shut it off. He didn't know what to say to her. A moment ago he was going to tell her he'd seen the light, he was going to turn away from the alchemy of turning life into literature, of treating reality as the raw material for something more refined, he would stop having fictitious affairs with waitresses and barmaids, he would stop agonising over the *mot juste*. He would, in short, say nothing. He would just be. But that was then and this was now.

He went back to the hotel, changed out of his wet things, asked the barman for a large whisky and sat at the bar reading his messages. There were two messages from Daniela saying she'd tried to call. He called her.

We got cut off, Daniela said. Then when I tried to call you were engaged.

It was the BBC. They've invited me on to The Book Program.

Oh, how exciting. You said yes, I presume. I'm so pleased for you.

Thanks. I didn't know anything about it. I'd switched my phone off. I've been thinking about what you said, about living in the moment, about nowness.

Oh, and?

Nothing really. Nothing conclusive, anyway, except that by turning my phone off I missed a rather important now moment.

He laughed when he said it but the laugh sounded hollow. He was lying to her or, if not lying, not entirely truthful. He'd already decided to withhold the information about his epiphany. The epiphany had been cancelled, annulled or, at the very least, put on hold. As for living in the moment, this was it; his moment had come.

Are you OK? Daniela said. It was impossible to keep anything from her; she had an ear for the unspoken.

Yeah, I'm fine. Changed out of my wet things.

There was a long silence. He sensed Daniela leaning into the silence, interrogating it.

Earlier, when we got cut off you were saying that you'd decided something.

Did I? I don't remember. I think I was babbling a bit. I'm still reeling from the news.

I bet.

There was a reproach wrapped up inside the words that said, I know you're not being straight with me.

So, how much longer do you plan to stay?

I won't be staying. I'll fly back tomorrow. Can't waste my time here. I need to get down to work, now this has happened. Seb will want to know about work in progress, irons in the fire and all that.

I'm glad. I'll cook us something nice, to celebrate. Have you got any ideas?

Up to you. You're the chef.

I meant any ideas about what to write next.

He didn't have much in the way of ideas. What he had was some great first lines, or he thought they were great, but nothing more. One began: Closure? Don't talk to me about fucking closure. He had no idea what might come next.

Dunno, he said. There's the story I've been working on. You said you liked it.

The one about the barmaid you want to sleep with except her husband is a cop, that one?

Yes. I've only written a couple of scenes so far. Not sure where it's going.

He was already musing about a story about someone who is lost for words or maybe lost in words. Perhaps his epiphany could be the starting point of something. He wanted to get off the phone so he could start making notes.

Are you still there? Daniela said. See you tomorrow?

Sorry, my head's all over the place. I'll message you when I'm on the plane. Love you.

Love you, too. Safe journey.

Victor

We need to talk about Paula.

When do we talk about anything else?

She's sixteen, it's problematic.

That's one way of putting it.

Their daughter's current frame of mind could be summed up as fuck you, fuck everyone, I hate my fucking life.

Seriously. I think she needs help.

You mean we do.

That attitude isn't helpful.

Sorry, but I can't talk now. I have to go to work. Saul's called a meeting.

Is that such a big deal?

For Saul, yes.

OK, off you go. Are you OK?

What do you mean?

Lately you've seemed, I don't know, anxious, preoccupied.

Really? I'm fine.

Esther put a hand on his shoulder and looked him in the eye.

You would tell me, wouldn't you? If something was wrong.

Of course, I would, Victor said, kissing her lightly on the lips.

And he would. He will. Just not yet.

When Victor stepped outside the building the air was thick with heat. The street shimmered and throbbed. The sky was that tell-tale billiard chalk blue that heralded another furnace of a day. Sweat dripped down his spine and gathered in the waistband of his underpants. Now he was going to have to sit in his damp clothes in a freezing cold conference room. Saul liked the air con turned up high.

The young woman who begged outside the supermarket was there, wearing that mournful look, like a character in a Polish art house movie. He avoided her eyes. She made him uncomfortable. He didn't like to see her there, so vulnerable. It seemed all wrong. But he never gave her money, nor to any of the other beggars. There were so many now. He didn't see the point; what difference would a few coins make? It was just conscience-salving. It didn't do any good.

People drooped visibly in the swamp-like humidity of the metro station. Then when the train arrived it was like stepping into a fridge. One passenger was reading a book, everyone else was looking at their phones. Victor was trying to wean himself off his and was relearning how to live in his thoughts. But his phone beeped, once, then repeatedly. That would be Saul. Saul was one of those people who hits send every three or four words so that instead of receiving one message you get ten. It was irritating but Saul had his ways and he wasn't about to change.

The messages were all about the Dubai contract, of course, which was what the meeting was about too. Saul couldn't talk about anything else. Dubai, he kept saying. This is the big one, Victor. This is a game changer.

Whenever anyone asked Victor, so what do you do? he paused, though not for effect.

I'm in paint. That's what he always said. I'm in paint, and watched as the blankness spread across their face like a light fall of snow.

Not house paint, he'd add. Paint for bridges, steel structures, ships. I know what people say, as interesting as watching paint dry. It's true, watching the stuff dry is pretty dull. But paint is interesting. To me it is, anyway.

Victor's background was in chemical engineering. He understood paint, Saul just sold it. Saul liked to say, I talk shit and Victor talks science. That's why we're such a great team. Saul had a line in self-mockery that boosted his ego. Look what a great guy I am, I take the piss out of myself even in front of my staff. It worked. Saul was the first man Victor had met who used bonhomie as a form of intimidation.

Victor sat on the metro reading Saul's messages. It was all about strategy and preparing for the conference call with the client, a shipowner in Dubai. The conference call would be in English. Saul's English was OK but he was afraid of making a fool of himself so he always got Victor to front the meeting. Victor was working on his shipping vocabulary in anticipation. Lately he'd been practising how to say the word hull, but it still came out as either hall or hole.

Here he is, the man who knows. Saul clapped his hands together when Victor walked into the meeting.

That was his catchphrase for Victor, the man who knows. Victor was what Saul called a details guy. Saul divided the world between details guys and big picture guys. He, needless to say, was a big picture guy. Information is power, that was another of his catchphrases. Hardly a day went by that he didn't pull on that lopsided smile of his, widen his eyes and tap the side of his nose and say information is power, like he'd just coined the phrase. He didn't dig out the information himself, that was too boring. He relied on the details guys to do that, people like Victor. Without Victor, everything would be left in the air, dangling, as Saul lost interest and moved on to the next thing. But it was Saul who got the glory, he made sure of that. Victor was forever the bridesmaid but that was OK, he didn't mind. Not everyone wants to be the bride.

Saul was one of those people you don't have to like but you can't help but admire. He had chutzpah and charm in large and equal measure. He was a showboater and a loudmouth and a bullshitter. That is, he let people think he was. It was the old hustler strategy; convince people they're better than you, let them think you're dumb and they're getting the better of you, then, when you see that look of triumph in their eyes, reel them in.

He was also a control freak and like control freaks the world over he couldn't cope with the state of unknowing. He was impatient. It wasn't the run-of-the-mill impatience like when the train's late or you're waiting for the band to come on; the impatience of wanting things to begin. Saul wasn't impatient for things to begin but rather for them to end, because once they end the next thing can start.

When I read a thriller, the first thing I do is read the last few pages, he told Victor once.

But that just spoils the whole thing. The whole point of a mystery is that it's a mystery.

I know, but I have to know how it ends. Otherwise, I can't bear the suspense. Then I can start at the beginning and relax.

Victor got along with Saul professionally. They made a good team. On a personal level he found him a bit too overwhelming, too in your face. Victor was a quiet, thoughtful guy but Saul was one of those people who absorbs all the available light. He held court, always the centre of attention, forever joking around with his exhausting and inexhaustible bonhomie. He was full of praise for Victor.

Victor is brilliant, he told people. Without him the business would fall apart.

But the way he said it, rather than boost Victor's self-esteem, it had the opposite effect. It made Victor feel small. It felt like Saul was mocking him. And yet he wanted, even craved, Saul's approval. It was like being back at school. He longed for an encouraging word from his teachers but praise wasn't in the school's ethos. Pupils were encouraged to do better by being told they had done badly. Praise was seen as a sign of weakness.

When Saul discovered Victor's wife Esther was a graphic designer he hired her to do some work on the company's website. Victor was uneasy about mixing his home and working life but Esther and Saul seemed to hit it off. They both liked to flirt in a way that didn't mean anything, it was just play.

He's full of piss and wind and is really quite ridiculous, but he makes me laugh, was her verdict. If someone makes me laugh, I can forgive a lot else about them.

So, Saul said theatrically. Here's the thing.

He paced the room. Everyone else was sitting around the table, leaning back in their Eames chairs. Saul's courtiers.

Five ships, three million each. So that's fifteen mil for a start. Then there's the maintenance contract. That's worth another ten or twelve mil over ten years. This contract alone could keep us all in work for the next five years. But first we have to get it, right?

Right, said the room. Saul liked this sort of call and response stuff. Team building, he called it.

This is a three-way fight. We're up against R&J and, as always, the Danes. R&J are already connected in Dubai. As for the Danes, you know we can't compete on price, so it has to be something else. So, gentlemen, what can we offer that they haven't got? What's our USP?

Quality, someone piped up.

Correct. Ka-wality. But so what? Quality is all very well but not if the price is too high.

Longevity, Victor said.

Longevity, says the man who knows. My man Victor, the only person in this company who's allowed to use words of more than three syllables. Tell us, Victor, why does longevity matter?

A huge bee buzzed against the window, trying to get in. Victor watched as it bashed frantically against the glass.

Victor? Are you with us?

Yes, sorry. Longevity means less maintenance which means longer between repaints, so less time the ship is out of action.

Less time the ship is out of action. And there you have it, boys and girls. Spend more on paint and your ships are at sea longer so you make more money. There's your USP right there.

Victor was having trouble maintaining his focus. His mind kept going back to what the doctor said about the endoscopy. There's a vocabulary you acquire over time, words you have no need of when you're young, words like tumour, sarcoma, malignant, benign, remission, metastasis. Endoscopy. When you get past forty these words keep cropping up in conversation.

He hadn't said anything to Esther. She'd only worry.

It's probably nothing, the doctor said. But we'd like to do an endoscopy. Just to be sure.

As it turned out, the doctor was wrong; it wasn't nothing. The news was bad but the doctor insisted it wasn't that bad. You have to look at it in the round, he said. The round, as he put it, looked something like this: radiotherapy to shrink the tumour and then chemo. It's about management, he said. What this translated as was: make no mistake, this thing is going to kill you; it's a question of when. Five good years, maybe more. He didn't say how many bad ones, nor did he offer a definition of a good one. Victor had seen friends on chemo. It looked hellish, and they said, yes, it was, but still better than the other option. So, the good years would include feeling sick as a dog on chemo while watching his hair fall out. Still, five years was five years. A friend of a friend went to the doctor with a pain in his lower back and six months later he was dead. Five years was better than six months. Victor was looking for the upside.

He was due to start treatment in a week and he still hadn't told Esther. The Dubai meeting had been brought forward. He was flying out the next day. If he didn't tell her today it would have to wait till he got back, the day before treatment began.

He took Esther out for dinner in an Italian restaurant Saul recommended. He should have known. It was all bling and gilded mirrors and naked statuettes and busts of Roman emperors alongside gilt-framed signed photographs of Dean Martin, Donatella Versace and Salvatore Schillaci. There were linen table cloths and napkins and the tables gleamed with heavy cutlery and more glasses than anyone could use, most of which the waiter removed once they'd ordered. The chairs wore covers as though out of modesty, chairs that the waiter made a great show of orchestrating as he sat Victor and Esther at their table. Whatever the intention, the place had the flavour of ancient Rome meets the New Jersey wise guys.

They'd finished the starter and Victor was still no closer to knowing how he was going to tell Esther his news.

Esther raised her glass.

Good luck tomorrow, she said. How are you feeling about it?

OK, not as well prepared as I'd like to be. I'm more worried about my English than anything else. All these words about ships. The front of a ship is called the bow.

The what?

Bow. The teacher said, you know, bow wow, like a dog, and I said what do you mean, that's not the sound a dog makes. It's the sound it makes In English, he said. Imagine that, the same dog sounds different in English.

Esther laughed. The English like to be different. You'll be alright, she said.

Their starters arrived, insalata caprese for her and something with burrata for him. The waiter filled their glasses.

I hate it when they do that, Esther said after he'd gone. I'm a big girl, I can fill my own glass.

You know what Saul is most excited about with this trip? Victor said, procrastinating. His air miles. He's obsessed with air miles. He'll take any trip with the company just to accumulate air miles. It's that something-for-nothing mentality of his. If the drink's free he'll drink it, even if he doesn't want a drink. He never normally eats breakfast, just a cup of coffee. But when he stays in a hotel he grazes the breakfast buffet - yogurt, fruit, bacon, scrambled eggs – you name it. Just because it's free. Which it's not, of course, it's all been paid for. He says after this trip he'll have enough air miles for a free flight to Miami.

Miami would be right up his street, I imagine. Like this restaurant, cheesy and fattening.

Victor needed to tell her the truth about his health but shield her from that truth too. He didn't want to make her feel bad. It's one thing to share your sorrows, another to dump them on others. Of course, he had to tell her, she'd find out soon enough anyway, but he couldn't see a way to sweeten the pill. He thought it might be easier if they went out, which was why they were having dinner in this absurd wedding cake of a restaurant, but each time he lined up the words, there's something I need to tell you, the words backed off.

The waiter brought the main courses which, although they'd ordered different dishes, looked remarkably similar, differently shaped pasta struggling to stay afloat in a heavy sea of cheese sauce.

They both giggled over the Italian waiter performance with the parmesan grater and the giant pepper mill. He attempted to refill their glasses but Esther put a hand over her glass and said with the sweetest of crocodile smiles, leave it to me. Miffed, the waiter flounced off with a resentful *prego*.

We need to talk about Paula.

Victor sighed.

Here we go, he said.

Lately they rarely saw eye to eye about their daughter. But at least talking about Paula was an excuse not to bring up the C-word, which was a relief. Victor wound some pappardelle round his fork. The sauce was gorgonzola and cream. Pure heart attack, he thought, then laughed to himself. A heart attack is the least of your worries, he thought.

I know you think I'm being hysterical, but I really think we need to do something.

I don't think you're being hysterical, I've never said that. Just that we have to be patient. She's sixteen; think of it as an illness. She'll get better.

Easy for you to say. With you she's daddy this and daddy that, but I'm the evil bitch from hell. The names she calls me: stupid, stupid cow, stupid old cow, fucking stupid old cow – like she's conjugating a verb.

Victor laughed.

It's not funny.

No, it's not. But you are. And cow's a noun, not a verb.

Esther gave him slit eyes and eyed the pasta hanging from her fork, dripping five kinds of dairy.

This place, she said, in the sort of whisper you can hear at the back of the theatre. Do you think they're trying to kill us?

This was a cue for the waiter to sashay by and ask if they were enjoying their food.

Delicious, Esther smiled broadly. There was a spot of cheese sauce on her chin.

Seriously, though, I think Paula should see a psychologist, a psychotherapist, whatever. She's got a lot of issues, a lot of anger. I can't talk to her and you just think it's a phase, like bed-wetting. You do know she's talking about changing her name.

Really? Why? I thought she liked her name.

It's a binary name. It marks her out as a girl.

Paula is already the feminisation of a boy's name. And besides, she is a girl.

Not necessarily. Gender is a construct. Don't look at me like that. It's not that she wants to be a boy, she doesn't want to be locked into a gender identity. She says gender should be more fluid and frankly I think she has a point.

Fair enough. But whatever she calls herself, she's still a girl.

That's another can of worms. You don't want to go there, believe me.

So what do we have to call her now?

She hasn't decided yet. But please don't start making jokes about it. We have to be nice. This is a thing at the moment, all this stuff about gender; she's by no means alone.

I know. I'm not that out of touch. And if you think a psychologist would help, OK. Maybe that will take some of the heat off you.

Well, you've changed your tune.

Maybe, but it's Paula you have to convince, not me.

But you have to back me up. I need to know I can count on your support.

You know you can.

No, I don't. When the shit hits the fan, you run for cover. You don't back me up. Or not always.

I don't back you up when you lose your shit because she's left her dirty clothes on the bathroom floor because she can't find the strength to put them in the laundry basket. I don't back you up then because I think you losing your shit is worse than her being a lazy slob and I think sometimes you forget just who is supposed to be the adult in this situation.

Meaning I can't count on your support, she said archly.

Let's not do this, Esther. Yes, you can count on my support. But if you think she needs to see a psychologist, first find your psychologist. You know what happens, if you suggest something as an abstract idea she'll just say no before you've even finished talking. She'll probably say no anyway.

Yes, she probably will, and I do have a name, a woman someone recommended. She specialises in adolescents. But I need to be sure that when she goes running to you daddy, daddy, the wicked witch thinks I'm mad and she wants to send me away to the madhouse, you have to say the wicked witch is absolutely on point and I agree with every single word she says. Agreed?

Victor held up his glass. Agreed. The witch is wise.

Their forks lay idle in congealing puddles of gorgonzola, ricotta and cream. One waiter took their plates away while another de-crumbed the table cloth. They said no in unison to dessert or coffee or sambuca.

Shall we get a cab, or walk? Victor said when they were outside.

Let's walk. All those calories. I feel like a one-woman dairy farm.

Fucking stupid old cow, he said, taking her hand.

Don't you start, she laughed.

This was a fun thing to do, we should do this more often, he said, suddenly and acutely aware that often was not going to be what it used to be.

Yes, we should, she said. But in a different restaurant next time, please.

Victor wasn't going to tell her his news tonight. The mood was all wrong, the timing was wrong. This was a sweet moment; he felt close to her and knew she felt the same way. Why spoil it? He'd tell her when he got back from Dubai. But she must have sensed something was up.

Is there something bothering you? You seem a bit tense.

Me? No, I'm fine. Just the Dubai thing, you know, and my English.

You'll be OK, she said, giving his arm a squeeze. Just remember, bow as in bow-wow.

Yeah, right, like a dog. An English dog.

Late the following afternoon Victor was waiting at the airport security gate when Saul phoned.

Traffic's terrible and this idiot of a driver's taken a really stupid route. I'll be there as soon as I can.

Victor imagined the idiot of a driver overhearing this conversation, but Saul wouldn't care. He had that, I'm paying you so do your fucking job, attitude. Victor had another opportunity that morning to tell Esther his news over breakfast but then her mother called and that ate up the time before she left for work. It wasn't something he wanted to blurt out and then head for the airport. He wanted to protect her from bad news, not because she couldn't handle it but because he loved her and he didn't want to make her unhappy. Telling her he'd be dead in five years would make her very unhappy indeed.

Saul called again fifteen minutes later.

There's a fucking demo blocking the road. There's a load of riot police and they're not letting us move. We're completely stuck. You better go through security, just in case, and I'll meet you planeside.

Victor scanned his boarding pass and went through the security ritual: belt off, shoes off, pockets empty, mobile in the tray, laptop in a separate tray, wait obediently until he was waved through the scanner. It beeped, it always beeped for him. The guard frisked him, ran the body scanner over him, tested his hands for drugs and explosives. He assumed it would always be like this. One guy with some suspect fluid in a jar and another idiot with Semtex in his shoe and since then for billions of people it's been the same: belt off, shoes off, pockets emptied. Once we lose something, we never get it back. The days of just checking in and getting on a plane were gone forever.

Victor was drinking a cup of coffee he didn't really want when Saul called for the third time.

No way am I going to make it, he said. This is really fucked up. I'll get the first flight out tomorrow.

Victor's heart sank. There was only one flight a day, the one he was about to catch, which arrived in the evening. The presentation was in the morning. Saul wouldn't be there and he'd have to do the presentation without him. He needed Saul; Saul was the show.

Don't panic, Victor. I can hear you panicking. You'll be fine. I'll send you my bit of the presentation and the PowerPoint. Look them over when you get there. There's not a lot to it. Trust me, it'll be just fine. Anyway, you're the guy with the good stuff, the substance, the stuff that matters.

Victor had a childish desire to run away and hide until all this disappeared. People had no idea how shy he was. Every time he had to speak publicly or go to an interview he hoped something would happen that would prevent him from doing it, something out of his control, a *deus ex machina* that would give him the excuse to cancel.

He felt sick to his stomach. Saul was a clown and a bullshitter but Victor relied on him to front the show. He told jokes, he warmed everyone up and then Victor lulled them into submission with facts. If they were a rock band, Saul would be the lead singer, pacing the stage, soaking up the attention and bawling into the mic, and Victor the bass player, back there in the shadows, holding it all together.

The crew went over the safety chat as the plane taxied out to the runway. Once they were up and away and the seatbelt sign was turned off, Victor switched on his laptop and read Saul's presentation. There was no way he could do it. It wasn't just that Saul's English was shockingly bad, it was the style. Saul was a showman and Victor was not. The clients would think that Saul was a vulgar fool, which was what he wanted, but Victor couldn't pull that off. Victor didn't crack jokes; he didn't do the knowing self-mockery. He had to find a way of rewriting the pitch in his own words, otherwise he'd never be able to get behind it.

He had a window seat and a young woman in a hijab had the aisle. The middle seat, Saul's, was empty. When they took their seats Victor and the woman exchanged the nods, smiles and hellos that make it clear you're quite prepared to be pleasant but not in the least interested in striking up a conversation for the next seven hours.

About an hour into the flight, just as the drinks trolley appeared, the plane started to vibrate. At first it seemed like they were passing through a patch of turbulence but then it began to shake so violently that the trolleys were withdrawn and the seatbelt light was switched on. The crew hurried along the aisle making sure everyone was buckled up. The normally dull drone of the engines pitched up to a high whine. The cabin crew maintained an air of calm but discreetly exchanged nervous glances.

Victor's first thought was that if the plane had to turn back or land somewhere in Italy, which they were now overflying, he wouldn't be in Dubai in time to make the presentation, it would be postponed and then it could go ahead as planned, with Saul at the helm. Victor would be reprieved. The plane's mechanical failure was just the sort of *deus ex machina* he'd hoped for.

That was before the plane broke through the cloud cover and he could see the ground below. They were descending. They were still more than five hours from their destination and they were descending.

The anxiety spread through the passengers like a brush fire. There were a few muffled whimpers but mostly there was silence, the tense hush of people trying not to think the worst. The plane was still descending, slowly but definitely heading downwards. The tension broke into oh my gods and a few screams when the captain announced that we were going to have to make an emergency landing. Through the window Victor saw hills. A plane can't land on hills. Emergency landing was a euphemism for crash landing, or simply crash.

The woman in the hijab sat with her head down and her eyes closed. Her lips were moving and Victor thought she was praying. He considered putting a hand on her shoulder to comfort her but worried it might not be appropriate. Besides, what comfort could he offer; they were going to crash and almost certainly die. I am going to die, he thought, and then said, though he wasn't sure if he actually said it aloud, this is it, you're going to die.

Victor was afraid, of course he was. He was about to die and he didn't want to die. Who does? But here it was, the thing that was always coming was about to arrive. Death was right there, outside his window, in the green hills that seemed to rise up towards them. It was only minutes away. No sooner had he adjusted to the idea of riding cancer's slow train into the dark than here he was taking the express into green Italian hills. He wouldn't have to do Saul's part of the presentation nor his part either. They would never reach Dubai and the done deal would be undone. He wouldn't have to find a way to tell Esther about the cancer nor would he get the five good years the doctor promised. He wondered if someone else would get them, if that was how it worked.

When they called out Brace! Brace! over the PA. Victor felt an urge to giggle. He never imagined they said that in real life but a flight attendant hurried down the aisle ensuring that everyone adopted the brace position. Nearly everyone did as they were told. Victor understood immediately that telling passengers to adopt this position had nothing to do with surviving a plane crash.

It was to stop people panicking. It's physically difficult to scream in the brace position and bent double with your hands over your head you can't see the terror in your fellow passengers' eyes. It locks people into their private world of fear, avoiding the contagion of mass hysteria, like when small children hide their heads under a pillow, believing they've become invisible. There was some muted sobbing, but the passengers were mostly quiet, stunned into silence by the enormity of what was about to happen.

The flight attendant's professional mask of calm couldn't conceal the terror in her eyes as she moved down the aisle. She had melancholy, soft brown eyes. When she got to Victor, she gestured that he should adopt the same position as everyone else, but he shook his head. She seemed about to insist, caught between her training and the absurdity of the situation, as though putting your hands over your head would make the slightest difference when the plane plunged into the hillside. Her lips parted, but then she moved on, death in her lovely eyes, checking the other passengers.

The woman in the aisle seat was sobbing and praying. He reached over and took her hand. He felt a surge of love for her, a stranger but another human being and the person he was going to die with, not Esther or Paula or anyone else he knew and loved. They held hands across the empty seat between them and Victor felt a profound, visceral love and a sense of kinship for this fellow creature with whom he was sharing his final moments. It didn't matter who it was; it could have been anyone. There were no strangers now.

The engines were screaming now and the plane was vibrating so much it seemed about to fall to pieces. He thought about Esther and Paula. How would Paula react? Would this shake her out of her teenage solipsism or plunge her in deeper still? The world below came into focus, no longer the shapes and shadows of the aerial view. Victor could see houses, cars, some sheep in a meadow, smoke from a barbecue, a cycle race on a country road. He imagined the whirr of the peloton as it passed, that sound like a giant steel dragonfly. They were heading straight for the hillside. The plane had become a drawn-out, mechanical scream. The sheep scattered. The cyclists looked up at the sky. Victor didn't look away or close his eyes. The woman beside him squeezed his hand.

It's OK, he said quietly. Really, it's OK.

Esther had just got home when Saul called.

Amazing, isn't it, he said. Who else but Victor could pull off a stunt like that?

I don't know what you're talking about, Saul.

Victor. The plane crash. They're calling it a miracle. You don't know? Shit, sorry, I assumed you knew. Victor's plane crashed in Italy. But it's OK, don't freak out, he's OK. Totally amazing. Turn on CNN, it's on the news loop, they're showing it every five minutes.

Esther was too stunned to speak. She stayed on the line and turned on the television.

A TV reporter was standing in the middle of the road. Some way behind him there was an airplane. The reporter explained that the road was a stretch of the highway built along the route of the Via Appia in Lazio. This was where the plane made an emergency landing. Everyone on board survived and no one suffered anything worse than concussion, whiplash and, in one case, a broken arm. Several motorists were being treated for shock. Aviation experts described it as a miracle. The reporter turned to speak to someone. It was Victor.

Can you talk us through what happened? the reporter asked him.

The plane was descending fast, Victor said, his eyes flitting anxiously from the reporter to a point just past the camera. We were heading straight into a hillside and I thought, this is it, I'm about to die. We all did. There wasn't any other option. And then suddenly the hills were gone and there was a plain in front of us and a long straight road. It felt miraculous, like the parting of the Red Sea for Moses.

II have to say, you look like you've seen a ghost.

If I did, it was my ghost, Victor said with a laugh that got caught in his throat. I still can't quite believe I'm here talking to you. It doesn't seem possible. I was certain we were all going to die. No doubt at all. It was just seconds away. The pilot should get a medal. They should build statues to him. He's a total hero.

And what was …

But Victor ignored the reporter. He looked straight at the camera and said: Esther, I can't call you because I've lost my mobile, but if you're watching this, I love you. And you Paula. I'll be home soon. It's great to be alive. I can't tell you how great. Really.

There were tears in his eyes.

Oh, Victor, Esther said. Oh, my love.

Victor sat on the guardrail by the side of the road next to the women whose hand he'd held on the plane. He knew nothing about her, not even her name, but there was a bond between them. Together they had looked death in the eye and here they were, improbably, alive. Soon they'd go their separate ways, but the bond would always be there. He wanted to get home, to be with Esther and Paula, but he didn't want to fly. He didn't think he'd ever get on a plane again, so he'd probably never get to Dubai, whatever Saul said.

I've got cancer, he said to the woman.

She looked into his eyes and nodded slowly but didn't speak. Words were hard to come by and she, too, had seen her own ghost.

You're the first person I've told.

She took his hand and held it.

The doctor says I might have five years. Five good years, was what he said. It didn't seem like much until now.

She nodded again.

Life is a gift, she said. Every minute. Every second.

Kiss

Come on, let me stay. It'll be fun.

Joey lay on her bed, his hands clasped behind his head. It was a warm summer evening and he was dressed in shorts and a faded pink T-shirt. Skinny, barefoot, mussed up hair, olive skin, almond eyes, a tuft of dark air under his arms, a dirty smudge on his top lip, barely a rumour of a moustache. Still just a boy, really. Annemarie was more of a woman than he was a man; she had breasts, periods, they were the same age but he made her feel green and naïve. The way he said, it'll be fun, it was like he was goading her, challenging her to have fun, as though she didn't know how. Worse, he found her teddy bear under the pillow. She felt silly and girlish and embarrassed.

He was enigmatic; he liked to keep people guessing, cocky but funny, an androgynous Peter Pan who quoted Eliot and e.e. cummings and Dylan, both Thomas and Bob. If being enigmatic was designed to confuse, it worked on her. She liked him and she didn't. She wanted him to go and she wanted him to stay. He was arrogant, but there was also something sweetly boyish about him. And his mouth was an open invitation to a kiss.

Nothing's going to happen, you've got your chaperone, he said with a half smirk at her friend Jill, who was staying the night. Jill made eyes to ceiling and slid an LP out of its sleeve.

Annemarie looked at Jill who shrugged, as if to say, what do you expect me to do about this? Jill and Annemarie were best friends. Annemarie was pretty, Jill was not. Annemarie had thick, curly hair, big brown eyes and full lips. Jill's hair was straight and mousy, her eyes were small, her eyelashes were short and she had prominent eye teeth. Annemarie got a lot of attention from boys – and recently from men; Jill rather less. They had been friends since primary school and Jill didn't begrudge Annemarie her prettiness, who in turn never ceased telling Jill that she was attractive but that boys were too stupid and puerile to see it. Besides, there was solidarity between them on the boy front. They, like Joey, went to single-sex schools and until now had viewed each other as familiar but little-known species. Now both boys and girls had been swept ashore together on a gulf stream of hormones and neither knew how to behave.

Almost overnight boys became the dominant topic of conversation: who was fanciable, who was disgusting, who had gone how far, who had gone all the way. Annemarie had promised herself she'd stay a virgin until she was seventeen. It was an arbitrary choice but she suspected that once she crossed that line there was no going back. The idea of sex excited her, though when she imagined the act itself it seemed both gross and improbable. At a party she'd let a boy whose name she didn't know touch her through her bra, but that was as far as it went. Annemarie would be seventeen in six weeks' time. She found herself wondering if Joey would still be around then.

Why do you want to stay anyway? she said, doing her best to sound arch. Not that there's anywhere for you to sleep.

I like it here, he said, smiling. I like you.

The *you* was clearly singular, aimed only at Annemarie. This time it was her turn for eyes to ceiling, but she liked the sound of him saying he liked her.

Please, Joey said in a wheedling voice. I have no home to go to. I'm a poor orphan.

You do too have a home, Jill said tartly. And a good one too. Your mother's a QC, so don't come little orphan Joey with us.

She said *us* as a way of inserting herself back inside the you from which Joey had excluded her. Us meant her and Annemarie, not some Joey come lately.

There was a knock on the bedroom door. Annemarie widened her eyes and gestured frantically at the window. Her room gave on to the garage roof. Joey climbed out and crouched beneath the window sill.

Come in, Annemarie said just as Jill kicked Joey's ragged Converse sneakers under the bed.

I thought you girls might like some cake, Annemarie's mother said, following a plate of lemon sponge into the bedroom. Annemarie took the plate from her.

Thank you. I love lemon sponge, Jill said in a way that she knew sounded completely unnatural. Annemarie's mother picked up on it.

Is everything alright? she said, glancing around the room.

Of course, it is, mum. Just listening to music. Hot, isn't it?

Jill fanned her face with an album sleeve as if to make the point.

I know you girls are up to something, I can see it in your faces. But never mind, enjoy the cake.

Once she'd gone they went to the window. Joey was lying on his back under the sill, wearing a big grin.

Coast clear? he said.

That was close. You've really got to go. You're going to get me into trouble.

Joey's response was to climb back into the bedroom. He sat cross-legged on the end of her bed. He broke off a piece of cake and stuffed it in his mouth.

Hmm, homemade. Really good.

It wasn't for you, actually, Jill said, turning the record over.

A song went by.

I could sleep on the floor. It's so hot, I won't even need a sheet.

What makes you think we want you to stay?

There's no need to get so uptight, Jill.

She was about to stick her tongue out but stopped herself. It would have looked childish. Jill aspired to be sophisticated. Whatever Annemarie said, she knew she wasn't pretty, so she strove to be interesting. She wore black, she read Proust and Doris Lessing; when Joey misquoted *The Waste Land* she corrected him.

Another song was playing; Janis Ian's *At Seventeen*. Annemarie knew she should have defended her friend, insisted that she wasn't the slightest bit uptight, but it took the pressure off her. If he called Jill uptight, by implication Annemarie was not; she didn't want Joey to think she was uptight too.

I'm going to the loo, Jill said.

The moment Jill shut the door Joey got up from the bed and stood in front of Annemarie. She had butterflies in her stomach and her pulse accelerated. He touched her cheek then twined one of her curls around his finger.

I want to kiss you.

She looked away, because she didn't know where to look or what to do with her face. He waited until she looked him in the eye.

If you kiss me, I promise I'll leave.

Only later did this strike her as a peculiar bargain. After all, if she kissed him, she'd most likely want him to stay so she could kiss him some more. On the other hand, he really did have to leave.

He tilted his head to one side and moved his face closer to hers. She closed her eyes, then opened them when his lips touched hers. It wasn't her first kiss, kissing was the one thing she'd done a lot, or at least quite a bit, but so far it wasn't all it was cracked up to be. Jill's big sister, who was twenty-one and therefore the oracle on the topic of boys and men, said that when it came to kissing men basically fell into two categories: spaniels, who slobber all over your face, and wolves, who seem intent on devouring you.

Joey was gentle and kissed her slowly, not ramming his tongue against her teeth before she was ready, but brushing his mouth against hers until her lips parted of their own accord. Lips and tongue were merely a starting point. The kiss went through her, shimmering in her blood, luminous, deliquescent, at once raw and soothing, a delicious tide flowing from shore to shore of her being. It was just a kiss, he didn't put his hand up her shirt the way other boys did, as though you wouldn't notice just because you had your eyes shut. He cupped her head in one hand while the other rested on her shoulder. He kissed her as though he adored her, as though there was no one in the world he'd rather kiss. It wasn't sex, it was a kiss, but even so it marked a before and after. She'd crossed the line.

The kiss lasted the entire song and, just as it was fading, through the thin walls came the sound of the toilet flush. When Jill came back into the room they had already separated, but it was obvious from their glow that something was going on. Jill raised her eyebrows at Annemarie who returned the look with a goofy smile.

Oh, Jill said.

I was just leaving, Joey said, taking a step towards the door.

But you can't go out the front, Annemarie said. They don't know you're here. They'd kill me if they knew you were up in my room. I'll be grounded for weeks.

Joey climbed on to the garage roof and looked down. It was about a ten-foot drop to the ground.

You can do it, Jill said with a malicious smile.

See you, then, Joey said. He sat on the edge, braced himself with both hands and jumped. He cried out when he landed and then he was gone.

When Annemarie saw him at the bus stop the next day his ankle was strapped up and he was on crutches.

Oh my God, she said.

It's OK. Sprained, not broken. The worst bit was I had to hop all the way to casualty.

Hopalong Cassidy, Jill sniggered. Annemarie shot her a look.

I'm so sorry, Annemarie said. I mean it, I really am.

It's OK, don't worry about it. Besides, it was worth it.

Annemarie blushed, not at the memory because it wasn't yet a memory: the kiss was still there, quivering inside her.

That was thirty-five years ago. Nothing came of that kiss and a few months later Joey left school and moved away. She never heard from or about him and he hadn't crossed Annemarie's mind in years – decades – until just now, when she stepped out for coffee to escape the solipsism of home working, that vague sense of irritation and even vaguer sexual fantasies that come from spending too much time in your own company. After she was made redundant she went freelance but newspaper journalism now paid so badly she had to diversify. She adapted, trading on her newspaper experience to attract other, less glamorous clients.

Her office had once been the baby's room and there was still a mobile of paper birds hanging from the ceiling that she hadn't got around to taking down. She was putting together a piece for the European fisheries commission's website on the new restrictions on catches of pelagic fish. She had to look up pelagic. Every month the agency that handled the Commission's media sent her some links that combined European decrees with quotes from the commissioner and maritime experts. Her job was to put it all together in such a way that someone might actually want to read it. Just sex it up a little, Annemarie, was the mantra from her contact at the agency.

So, to take a break from her own company and sexing up pelagic fishing quotas, she went down to her local café and what was playing but Janis Ian's *At Seventeen*, the very song that provided the soundtrack to her kiss with Joey. Her friend Jill played it over and over. She identified with the song, which was addressed to ugly duckling girls like me and those of us who knew the pain of Valentines that never came. But it struck a chord with Annemarie as well, even though she was one of the pretty girls who win the game. The song captured perfectly the confusion and drama of being a teenage girl.

The memory of the kiss was intense, visceral. Annemarie closed her eyes and let the song take her back inside her sixteen-year-old self, the hot summer evening, the waft of freshly mown suburban lawns, Joey with that why not, anything goes mien of his, and that kiss – rhapsodic, symphonic. It shone in the memory like mercury. She had a son of 16, the same age as Joey was then. Curious to think her son might have that sort of power, that sexual charge, that he might be capable of causing such havoc in a young girl's heart. She couldn't see it, but then she was his mother. How could she possibly know?

Back in her office she saved the pelagic fishing file to her desktop and Googled Joey Tulloch. There were a dozen. She tried to imagine what had become of him. She tried some social media sites, hoping for a photo, but no luck. She began a process of elimination. One was a country singer and another ran a transport and logistics business, neither of which sounded like Joey. She hesitated over the colour therapist but put him on the B list, as she did with the one who was president of the Moray Historical Society in Elgin. Eventually she whittled it down to two: one worked in something called opinion analytics, the other had been arraigned in a north London court on charges of possession of two kilos of cannabis, more than could be considered for personal consumption. She could find no record of his being sentenced.

She chose the opinion analytics Joey over the dope dealer for the simple reason that she found an email address for the former. The entire process had put her into a state of girlish excitement that she hadn't experienced in a long time. She hadn't thought about this man – this boy – in decades and suddenly she was possessed with the idea of meeting him. For what? To do what? To say what? She had no idea, but before she succumbed to doubt she wrote: You probably don't remember me. When you were 16 you sprained your ankle when you jumped off the garage roof so my parents wouldn't find you in my bedroom. Annemarie. She didn't mention the kiss. After all, he might not remember. She closed her eyes and pressed send.

Three days passed during which Annemarie revisited the teenage agony of waiting for a longed-for phone call. She told herself not to be so silly, it was all just a fantasy and that if she ached for anything it wasn't Joey Tulloch but her younger, less complicated self, or that she simply spent too much time in her own company and needed to get out more. But all that was in her head, it was rational, and this was coming from another place, the place that is home to love and desire and infatuation, the place of anxious, mouth-drying, stomach-churning excitement. There was no mistaking it.

It was while trying to dream up an eye-catching headline on Polish fish farming than an email from jmtulloch arrived with a pop. She resisted the temptation to open it immediately. Maybe it would say, sorry, I've no idea who you are. She tried to focus on the headline but the associations that arose were totally inappropriate. The Poles farm carp and a succession of carping on and carp about ideas suggested themselves. It was useless. There was nothing for it; she opened the mail.

It read: Hi Annemarie. Sure, I remember. How are you and where? Sorry not to get back sooner, I was on the road. Cheers. Joe.

So, no longer Joey. Perhaps he'd grown out of the boyish diminutive. But she didn't buy the bit about not getting back because he was on the road. Everyone was connected 24/7. No, it took him three days to decide to respond. So now what? The ball was in her court. He didn't say, I'd love to meet up, just how and where are you.

She didn't reply immediately. She didn't want him to think she had nothing better to do, so she waited a few hours before she wrote: Phew, I was worried I might have got the wrong Joe. Good to hear from you. I'm in London, keeping busy. You?

That was enough information, no specifics about her job, kids, marital status. Let him make the running. Annemarie, she said out loud. You are being unbelievably childish. And she was, but it was exciting. It was the mystery, the frisson that comes from anonymity. After all, aside from that kiss, they were perfect strangers.

He replied immediately: Such a long time. I'm not in touch with anyone from those days. I'm in London too. Maybe a drink some time?

There it was, an invitation. Her immediate reaction was do I want to go through with this? to which she countered, go through with what? A week later Annemarie was flipping through the hangers in the wardrobe. She had no idea what to wear. What did she want to say about herself? She didn't know because she didn't know whom she was meeting. It was like a blind date but without the romantic angle. At least, it wasn't intended to be romantic, but ever since she Googled Joey's name she was like a person possessed. She hardly thought about anything else, could barely concentrate on her work, even forgot all about her daughter's school concert and arrived ten minutes from the end.

She looked in the mirror. She was wearing black jeans, a floral patterned shirt and purple Reeboks. Fuck it, she said to her reflection, go as you are. You look fine. It's not a date after all.

There's lasagne made, she said. Her son was stretched out on the sofa immersed in his phone. Her daughter, also staring at her phone, sat side on in an armchair. You just have to heat it up. And there's salad.

Her son didn't react, quite possibly didn't hear her.

Are you sure you're wearing enough perfume?

Her daughter, who was fourteen, had recently discovered sarcasm and was still punishing her mother for missing her concert. She could pull a sulk for a week. At least with the boy it was all over in a moment. My life is shit! he'd scream. I hate this fucking family. Cue bedroom door slamming and half an hour of full-volume gangsta rap, but that was him done. It was like a bomb going off. Not so her daughter. Annemarie once saw a nature program in which a pair of small reptiles put their venomous bite into a water buffalo and then sat waiting and watching for the three days it took the beast to die. That was her daughter's style.

Love you, mum, her son called out as she left the room, apparently having taken everything in through his third eye.

Love you both lots, she called over her shoulder.

Joey-Joe said he worked in the West End and suggested they meet in a tapas bar in Soho, giving them the option to eat if they wanted. A tapas bar seemed a bit naff but she said nothing and told herself not to pre-judge. Annemarie arrived dead on time so she walked around the block until she was ten minutes late. The place was packed and she scanned the room for a single man. A voice called out. Annemarie? He was behind her, at a corner table by the window. He stood up and took her hand and in the same action took her elbow and drew her towards him so he could kiss her cheek.

He was dressed in jeans, T-shirt and a cotton jacket and was fashionably unshaven. He still had most of his hair, mostly grey, cropped short. He smelled nice, not of anything in particular, just a good clean man aroma. He was heavier, inevitably, but not in bad shape. His face had filled out and he had the jowly look of a drinker. He flicked his eyes over her as she sat down. Thirty-five years and two kids later this wasn't the girl he once held in his arms but she was pretty good for her age, she thought, with her clothes on, at least.

You recognised me, just like that.

There's a picture of you online.

Oh my God, my picture byline. That was taken ages ago.

You haven't changed much. Since the picture was taken, I mean.

Flattery, she noted. The picture was at least ten years old and even then she'd got a guy on the picture desk to Photoshop out her frown lines.

She tried to match the Joey in her head with the Joe before her. Not having witnessed any of the transition from youth to middle age, it was quite a jump. She imagined he was thinking much the same thing about her. She scanned his face for the teasing boy who lay on her bed with his hands behind his head. He wasn't there. Joe and Joey were, in effect, different people. It was the change in his eyes that struck her. Joey's eyes were full of mischief, mocking and self-mocking. The mischief had gone to be replaced by something sorrowful but also, she resisted the word but it stuck: seedy. There was definitely something a bit seedy about Joe.

Annemarie considered herself socially adept. She knew how to oil the wheels, keep the conversation going, get people talking to each other. She took pride in being able to winkle words out of the most monosyllabic men. It was easy really, you just got them to talk about themselves. But sitting with Joe she was struggling to find a way to first base. From the moment she sent the email she'd allowed a sixteen-year-old Annemarie to take the emotional helm but as soon as she sat down opposite Joe she ran aground on her fifty-one-year-old self. The almost dizzying excitement she'd felt ever since she Googled his name had ebbed away and left her feeling flat, a little foolish and uncharacteristically lost for words.

So, he said, arching an eyebrow. So many questions, but where to begin?

The question she really wanted to ask was what were you doing in my room? Aside from the kiss, all she remembered was that he was in her room that one time. Even back then they didn't even really know each other. They were never part of the same crowd, they didn't hang out together, which made her wonder how he came to be there at all.

We could make it like an application form, I suppose, he said. Marital status, children, place of work, chronic health problems, allergies, criminal records, stations of life sort of thing. Though maybe that would be boring, he added defensively when she didn't respond.

The waitress appeared, electronic notepad in hand. Thin-lipped, grey eyes narrow and welcoming as gun slits. Polish, almost certainly, Annemarie thought, thinking of carp farming. They hadn't looked at the menu. The waitress puckered her unpainted lips, not bothering to disguise her irritation.

Hungry? Joe asked.

Not really. A nibble perhaps. You go ahead and order, I eat everything.

He looked up to give his order but the waitress had gone.

Charming, Annemarie said.

Let's get a drink at least, he said, with his hand in the air, trying to attract attention

Beer, wine, water? What do you fancy?

Wine, please.

Red or white?

Red.

Eventually the waitress came over and he ordered a bottle of wine.

I'm a journalist, she said, just to break the ice. Twenty years on Fleet Street, as we used to call it. Ten at the *Independent*. I'm not there any more. Hardly anyone is. It's pretty much over for newspapers as we know them. I've been freelance for years now. I do everything – business, fashion, travel, culture, book reviews, restaurant reviews, fish – you name it and I'll deliver one thousand plausible, litigation-proof words by deadline. Gun for hire, that's me.

Fish?

Yeah, fish. Trust me, you don't need to know the details.

The waitress brought the wine and a basket of bread. She popped the cork, dropped it into her apron pocket and poured the wine without offering them a chance to taste. Everything about her said she didn't want to be there. Joe said he wanted to order some tapas. The waitress sighed, fished the notebook from her apron and took the order, petulantly stabbing the screen with her finger

She's fun.

An absolute poppet, Annemarie said, but at least the waitress had given them something to bond over. The tension eased. They raised their glasses.

Good to see you, whoever you are, he said with a smile. She liked the smile and was beginning to warm to him.

Yes, cheers to whoever we are, she said. So, your turn, tell me something about you.

Not married, never have been. Not in a relationship. One kid, a boy of twenty.

Interesting, she thought. I tell him about my work and he tells me about his personal life; a bit of role reversal. She liked the fact he had a son; it was a point of affinity. It made him a fellow member of the parent tribe; they spoke a common language. Several of her women friends were childless. It was a sensitive area and she had learnt to self-censor, not to go on about what her kids were doing or moan about how they were driving her crazy.

She tried not to but she was already calibrating Joe, ticking boxes: has kids Yes/No, likes music Yes/No, sense of humour Yes/No, good teeth Yes/No.

I'm happily divorced. Two kids, a boy of sixteen and a girl of fourteen.

That sounds like fun.

Fun? Yeah, really you can't imagine how much, living with two people who never tire of telling you how useless and stupid you are. No, really, it's not that bad, we get along well most of the time, we even have fun. But you know what it's like with teenagers. Total minefield. You must be through all that by now, twenty's pretty grown up.

Yeah.

The yeah was opaque, but she got the message: change the subject.

So what's opinion analytics, that's your field, right, Joe? It's Joe now, not Joey?

You can call me Joey if you like. No one's called me that in a long time. What do I do? I'm sort of a spy, a digital spy. I set up a small company and businesses and organisations hire us to find out what people are saying about them online. We designed some software that filters out most of the junk. If a company launches a new product or the government introduces a policy, we scan what people are saying about it and report back. It's like a focus group, but the net is a lot wider.

Annemarie's boredom alarm beeped. She didn't think social networks were as wonderful as people claimed. Most people don't have anything interesting to say. Before they had to fight to be heard; now they had blogs. A lot of the time it seemed like a global version of the guy who sits next to you on the bus and confides hush-hush how McDonalds is putting cocaine in its burgers so we all get addicted.

Really? I'd never have guessed that you …

That I'd turn into a nerd? Yeah, it's kind of nerdy. I

was surprised too. But that's the way it is. I had a friend who was a bit of a computer nerd. He was also a dope head, and he used to get stoned and write lines of code and he got me doing it. It's repetitive and mindless so it goes well with being stoned. Anyway, I discovered I was good at it. I started thinking and imagining things in code. It was like a gift.

Funny, isn't it, what you end up doing, things they never mentioned in careers advice at school. Jobs like yours that didn't even exist then. My best friend is a graphic designer. She worked with me on the Indy and we both got made redundant at the same time. Like me, she had to start hustling for work and she discovered, totally by chance, that she has a gift for dreaming up names for lines of lingerie. No, seriously. You can't market a pair of knickers just as knickers, they need images and names. She comes up with names like Silhouette or Dream Sequence or Degas. She's never worked in fashion but she has a knack for it and lingerie companies fly her to Paris, Madrid and New York and pay her good money to give presentations to their executives. People say don't leave things to chance but chance is what comes up with the goods in my experience. Like my friend, she has a gift she never knew she had.

He drank fast. He poured the last two glasses from the bottle and gesticulated for another. The waitress brought the wine and plonked the tapas down on the table. She might as well have been feeding the cat. Annemarie gave her a look but the waitress wasn't in the eye contact game.

That really pisses me off, that sort of attitude, she said after she'd gone. She may not want to be a waitress but right now that's what she is, so why can't she do her job with a bit of grace?

Maybe she's having a bad day.

We all have bad days. It doesn't mean you get to dump on everyone else.

Joe refilled their glasses. Annemarie was suddenly quite drunk. She often wondered why people look different when you're drunk, why they often seem more attractive. The wine was making Joe more attractive, but even drunk she was aware and wary of her attraction to men like him, men who seem a little damaged and wounded. You think you're the one, the balm for their aching souls, but when they're done with you it's you who needs treatment. It's like her friend Jackie said, you start out like Florence Nightingale, the ministering angel, and they leave you looking like Carrie.

So, are you happy Annemarie?

Now there's a question. Am I happy? Happiness is one of those things, isn't it, where you wouldn't turn down more were it offered. I'm not unhappy, and I look around me and I know I'm lucky. But I don't wake up singing, if that's what you mean.

I guess what I mean is have things turned out better or worse than you expected?

I'm not sure I remember what I expected. When you're young everything is so exciting. As time goes by things become more ordinary. Ordinary but also more precious - life, the living become more precious. When you're young you feel invulnerable. Now I'm more aware of the fragility of life. After all, you don't get to our age without chalking up some losses, do you?

That could have been a cue for him to talk about the son he didn't seem to want to talk about, or to reveal something else about himself, but he just nodded.

I would say that in the thirty-five years since we last saw each other I have gone from being a romantic girl to a sentimental woman. I don't know if that counts as evolution.

Which one sent the email, the romantic girl or the sentimental woman?

I suspect the romantic girl imagined she was making some sort of a comeback.

Seriously, why now? Don't get me wrong, I'm glad you did, just curious, that's all.

You just came to mind and I thought, I wonder what he's up to. I was bored, in my job I spend a lot of time on my own, so I Googled you. Don't tell me you never do that?

I check out people I do business with but otherwise, no. So, are you saying you remembered me for no reason, just out of the blue?

She had the feeling he was fishing but it wasn't clear what for.

Not quite. It was a song playing on the radio made me think of you. Janis Ian's *At Seventeen.*

I don't remember it. How does it go?

I'm not going to sing it for you, she said, a little more tartly than she meant to. If he didn't remember the song, had he also forgotten the kiss? And if he didn't remember the kiss, what was she doing here, since that was all there'd ever been between them? And really, what was she doing here? Chasing the sweet bird of youth? Did she imagine that by meeting Joe she'd enter a time machine and be sixteen all over again? She didn't want to be sixteen, she liked being the age she was. So what was she looking for? It was all about that kiss. There had been many kisses but that one kiss had a place of its own in her memory, a special place in her amorous trophy cabinet. So did she want him to say it was the same for him, that the kiss had lingered these thirty-five years? What did it matter if he did or didn't? The kiss was hers to keep.

Let's turn it around, she said. Why did you answer my mail? After all, it's not like we were ever even friends. There was just that one time that I recall.

Once again her tone was sharper than intended. She was annoyed, with herself and with him, as well as a bit drunk. He folded his hands and rested his chin on them; the thoughtful male pose, she thought unkindly.

Curiosity mostly. I didn't keep in touch with people from back then. We moved a lot when I was a kid, I guess I got used to being uprooted. I've never expected anything or anyone to last. I know people in their fifties who are still friends with kids they knew in primary school. I'm a bit envious of them, being able to go back that far, having that continuity in your life. I got your message and I thought, here's a bit of history I can reconnect with. Though I realise it's pure nostalgia, the idea of picking up the thread thirty-five years later, but I did remember you. I've even thought about you from time to time, wondered where you were and what you were doing, who you were with. Even though, like you say, there was just that one time. You know what I remember?

I'm all ears, she said, softer this time, feeling herself flush in anticipation of him mentioning the kiss.

When I jumped off the roof I knew it was too far down. I tried to sort of slide down the wall to break my fall but it wasn't enough. It hurt like hell but while I was hobbling and hopping away I thought of that stupid ad on TV when this guy dressed in black performs heroic feats in order to deliver a box of chocolates to a woman.

All because the lady loves Milk Tray.

That's it. Anyway, I thought of the ad and I just started laughing, because jumping off a garage roof was so anti-heroic compared to the guy in the ad who performs superhuman feats, leaping out of helicopters and over waterfalls. It helped me forget about the pain.

You forgot to leave the chocolates though, Annemarie said, cracking wise to disguise her disappointment that he hadn't mentioned the kiss.

The evening began to lose momentum. It was the second bottle slump, when you've drunk too much to keep up the repartee but not enough to do something you'll probably later regret. The conversation turned more banal. They talked about where they lived in London, property prices, how the city had become so expensive they could never afford to buy their flats now. Thank heaven our kids are nearly grown up or we'd be talking about schools, she thought. She mentioned a few people from the past but he didn't remember anything about them. He vaguely remembered Jill being in the room.

They finished the wine and got the bill. They went Dutch and Joe added a modest tip. Not that she deserves it, he said. They stood in the street, awkward. They'd had their reunion, now what? It was that blind date moment when you either arrange to see each other again or say something non-committal about how it would be nice to meet up sometime which you both know means goodbye. Once outside she realised that she was really quite drunk. She swayed a little.

It was a warm evening. The crowd spilled into the street outside the Dog and Duck, drinks in hand, laughing, smoking. A young guy in mirror sunglasses leaned against a white BMW talking to the driver, ignoring the beeping of the traffic backed up behind them. Two girls walking arm and arm bumped into Joe. One of them turned with a silly grin and coke-shiny eyes and started to apologise but giggled instead. Joe shrugged, then turned to Annemarie.

You haven't mentioned it but what I do remember is that we kissed, he said. Do you remember that?

I most certainly do. And I sincerely hope you haven't kissed anyone like that since.

He looked bemused. She giggled.

Just kidding, Joe.

There are very few perfect moments in life, Annemarie. His speech was a little slurred. That was one of them, so perfect that I began to wonder if I'd just dreamt it. Because I didn't know you, didn't know anything about you. I don't know what I was doing in your room. All I had was this fuzzy recollection of a girl called

Annemarie and a vivid memory of an amazing, extraordinary kiss. That was it. I couldn't remember anything else about you, I didn't know if there was anything else to remember. Then I got your message. You were real after all.

He moved closer to her, or did she just imagine that he did? Alarm bells rang. He was coming on to her. She'd sent him that email and he took it as an invitation, a come-on. Had he saved mentioning the kiss till now, right till the end, his seducer's trump card?

I've thought about you a lot, about that kiss, that moment. It's a mystery that nothing ever came of it. That kiss was something else.

This is the drink talking, Joe. It was just a kiss.

Having wanted him to remember and cherish it, now she wanted the kiss to herself. She didn't want to share it. She wanted to get away before he ruined everything by talking her into a drunken shag.

He looked into her eyes. His own eyes swam in alcohol. He cupped his hand around her head, poised to draw her into a kiss. That's when she remembered: Kiss me and I'll leave. That's what he said all those years ago. Suddenly she saw him, Joey emerging from under the carapace of Joe, the same boyish seducer, except sweet teenage Joey the androgynous flirt had grown into middle-aged Joe the pussy hound. Now it wasn't kiss me and I'll leave but let's fuck. That was OK, at her age it was good to know that anyone who wasn't deaf, dumb and blind still fancied her, even if they weren't exactly sober. But she wasn't interested. He pulled her towards him. She pulled away and put a finger on his lips.

I really don't think we could improve on the original, do you? she said in a stern, head teacher voice. He let his hand drop. He looked dejected, but not terminally so. He'd get over it pretty soon, she was sure of that. She looked at her watch. She was calling time on this little adventure.

I'm glad we met up, glad you remembered who I was, she said, her tone more placatory now. You're right, the kiss really was something special. Let's keep it that way. Why sour such a sweet memory with something as banal as reality?

A shame. Who knows, we may even have got better with time, he said, trying one last throw of the dice.

I doubt that very much.

She suddenly felt quite sober. She kissed him on the cheek. Take care.

It was unequivocally a goodbye kiss. If he was disappointed, he didn't let it show.

You too. It was nice to meet you.

See you around, she said. She turned and set off a little unsteadily in the direction of Soho Square. He hesitated, then headed off towards Shaftesbury Avenue. As he passed Ronnie Scott's he turned and watched her go. She didn't look back.

348 Grosvenor

When Marcos got home from school another woman was there instead of his mother. He called out, Hi, I'm home, but there was no answer. He dropped his school bag in the hallway and called out again, Mum, I'm home. Nothing. He went to the kitchen. Lately his mother had taken to spending a lot of time sitting at the kitchen table, chain-smoking Export A and drinking warm Coca-Cola. The ashtray on the faded yellow Formica was always full of lipsticked butts.

There was a woman in the kitchen but it wasn't his mother. She stood at the sink with her back to him, washing dishes. Maybe she hadn't heard him above the sound of the tap running. She had a large, soft body, not like his mother who was small and angular and fragile. The woman turned. She had a broad face and pink cheeks, fleshy, freckled arms and wavy, straw-coloured hair.

You must be Marcos, she said.

You're not my mother, he nearly said, but stopped himself because it was a stupid thing to say. She had a funny accent. He stood in the doorway and said nothing.

I'm Nancy, she said.

Where's mum?

She's not well.

He turned his head in the direction of his mother's bedroom.

Is she in her room?

No, she's not here right now. She's gone away but she'll be back, she said in a cheery way that was totally at odds with what she was saying.

When?

Oh, not for a little while, but don't worry, everything will be all right.

But where is she?

It didn't seem possible that she wasn't there. She was always there when he came home. She would put an arm around him and say, how was your day, schmutzig? Schmutzig was her pet name for him.

As I said, she's not well. She had to go away.

Away?

Yes. To hospital.

None of this made sense. If his mother was in hospital it must be something serious but from the way this woman acted it didn't seem serious. And who was she? What was she doing here? If his mother was in hospital, why wasn't his father there?

Is my father with her?

I imagine your father is at work.

Of course, he was, he was always at work. That's what fathers did. He knew all of his friends' mothers, almost none of their fathers. He looked round the kitchen. It was spotlessly clean. Only then did he realise it had been dirty for a long time. The table was sticky and there were always dirty dishes in the sink. The ashtray was always full and so was the garbage. Now everything was clean and there was no ashtray in sight. It was as though his mother had been removed; washed away. The woman took a step towards him. He felt sure she was going to touch him, give him a hug. He wanted to back away but he couldn't move. It was like one of those dreams when you're scared and want to run off but your legs are paralysed.

Just then the door to the apartment slammed. It was his sister. Every day she walked him home from school until they'd crossed Sherbrooke – that was the rule. But she'd often stop to talk to friends and leave him to go home alone because there were no more streets to cross. He shot her a look when she came in but she frowned because she didn't understand what the look meant. Nor did he really. She joined him in the kitchen doorway.

Hello, Janice, the woman said.

Janice didn't respond. She looked at her brother.

She says mum is in hospital.

Hospital! What happened?

She said this to Marcos, not the woman. Marcos shrugged.

Really, it's nothing to worry about, the woman said. Your mother is in good hands. Now how about I make you both a sandwich and then you can get on with your homework.

I don't have any homework, Janice said, petulant. Which hospital is she in?

I'm really not sure. You'll have to ask your father when he gets in. Now how about that sandwich?

Janice ignored her. She turned and pulled Marcos by the sleeve and took him down the corridor to her bedroom. She had her own bedroom; Marcos shared his with his brother Robert, the eldest of the three of them. Janice shut the bedroom door.

Who is that woman?

I don't know, she was here when I got home. She says her name is Nancy.

He felt accused, as though this was all somehow his fault. He thought he was going to cry.

I don't like her, his sister said.

Me neither, he said, and immediately felt better or, at least, not so alone.

Did she say why she was in hospital? Did she have an accident?

Marcos shook his head and then felt bad again, as though he should have asked more questions, but he was too confused.

She has a funny accent, he said, as though this information might be of use.

And she's fat, Janice added.

Janice had written I hate mummy in purple crayon on her bedroom wall after they'd had a fight. She started trying to rub it off but it just smeared so she covered it with a pillow. They sat close together on her bed, their arms touching. Their mother was there that morning when they left for school. She wasn't ill and she didn't say anything about going to hospital. Which meant it must have been an accident, but from the way that woman – that's how he thought of her, that woman, something inside told him not to call her by name – the way she talked it was like it was nothing serious or urgent, so what then?

Their mother had been different of late. She hardly cooked and there was never much food in the house and she seemed to exist on a diet of Carnation condensed milk, cigarettes and something called Veganin. He asked the man in the drug store what Veganin was and he said it was a painkiller. Sometimes she sent him out to the corner store for Cow Brand, which was a brand of bicarbonate of soda, sometimes for Export A, although now and then she switched to Du Maurier. He liked the red and gold packet. Instead of cooking their supper, more and more often she sent the three of them out to the drug store with five dollars for a cheeseburger and a milkshake.

There was a knock on the bedroom door. Janice didn't say come in and he didn't say anything either; it wasn't his bedroom. The door opened and the woman stood there with a plate of sandwiches.

I'm not hungry, Janice said, without looking up.

The woman ever so slightly raised an eyebrow then looked at Marcos.

Me neither, he said. It was a lie, he was starving.

Peanut butter and banana, the woman said, wiggling the plate, her voice rising on the word banana.

Janice didn't look up. Marcos stared at the radiator. About a month ago, when it was still cold enough to have the heating on, he shoved three brand new sponges down the back of the radiator in the hall. He didn't know why he did it but when his mother found them, gone hard and useless from the heat, she went mad. That was another thing, lately she lost her temper a lot. She shouted at them and even gave them the strap. Next time it'll be the buckle end, she'd shout. She never used to be like that. It was scary.

I'll just leave them here, then, the woman said, setting the plate down on the desk. After she left Janice got up and closed the door. He looked at his sister, then at the sandwiches.

Don't you dare, she said.

They sat and waited. Without saying so, they were waiting for Robert to come home. Maybe it wouldn't make any difference, but at least they'd all be there. Marcos tried to think about what had happened but, like moths against a streetlight, his thoughts just kept bashing into the one thing, his mother's unexplained absence.

Do you think it's because of that thing with the lawyer? Janice said.

Marcos shrugged. He didn't even want to think about that; he'd been trying his hardest to forget about it. About two months ago, he wasn't sure how long, but there was still snow on the ground, a man came to the house. They were all there in the living room, the three of them and their parents, who sat far apart from each other, their mother at one end of the sofa, and their father across the room on one of the dining room chairs. The man stood with his coat over his arm, a briefcase in his hand, like someone who isn't planning on staying long. Their mother explained that this man was a lawyer and he had a question to ask. She then looked at the lawyer, who cleared his throat.

What I'm here to ask you, what your parents have asked me to do, he said, addressing a point slightly above their heads, such that Robert even turned to see if there was someone else there, what they want me to ask is, if you had to choose who you would live with, your mother or your father, which would you choose?

Marcos didn't know how to answer such a question, or rather, he did, but he was afraid to. There was only one answer but it wasn't the right answer. There wasn't a right answer. He looked at the floor, only glancing up briefly to catch his mother's eye. His mother smiled emptily, an automatic smile that didn't seem to mean anything. His father glowered at the three of them. The lawyer shifted his weight from the coat side to the briefcase side, his face a question mark. The silence seemed to last forever.

Mum, Janice said, looking directly at their mother.

Me too, said Robert quickly.

Me too, mum, Marcos said, dry-mouthed.

The lawyer nodded, shifted his weight once more, and turned to the parents. Although he didn't move, you could sense him heading for the door. Their father got to his feet and nodded, which the lawyer took as a signal that he was free to go. The lawyer gave their mother a sort of half bow and turned to leave, their father at his side. Just as they were leaving the room their father turned to their mother with a look of total hatred.

Pig, he spat, and then left with the lawyer.

After that nothing changed, that is, they all continued to live under the same roof, and nothing more was said about it. Marcos wanted to talk to his brother and sister about it, he wanted reassurance, the sort of reassurance they might be able to offer because they were older than him. But Robert, as usual, shut himself away with a book or a car magazine while all Janice would say was why are they doing this to us, why are they being so mean?

Do you think it's our fault? Marcos said, wondering what he might have done to bring this down on their heads.

Don't be silly, she said.

But she didn't say it wasn't.

What did change was that after the lawyer's visit his mother stopped cooking and cleaning and spent her days at the kitchen table smoking and drinking warm Coca-Cola or evaporated milk from the can. One time he asked her what smoking was like. Go ahead and try it if you're so keen to find out, she said, passing him a lit cigarette. He held it between his fingers and put it between his lips.

Now what do I do?

Suck and inhale.

He did as she said and he immediately burst into a spluttering coughing fit. He thought he was going to be sick but instead of comforting him she laughed.

Now you know what it's like, she said as he wiped his eyes. So don't do it.

He didn't like the way she laughed. It wasn't a funny haha laugh, there was something mean about it, something cruel. She was never cruel.

At some point between the lawyer's visit and the arrival of the Nancy woman Marcos developed a habit of sitting on an armchair and rocking back and forward on the edge of the seat, all the while chanting tonelessly, bouncy-wounce, bouncy-wounce, bouncy-wounce. He could do it for hours on end. He found it comforting; it put him in a trance to the point where he felt nothing and was almost unaware of anything around him. But the others found it irritating and everyone – Robert, Janice, the Nancy woman and his father, if he was around – kept telling him to stop, which he did for a while but, without realising, he'd soon be rocking back and forth again, bouncy-wounce, bouncy-wounce, bouncy-wounce.

The first day the Nancy woman came to their house their father didn't come home. At dinner the four of them sat in silence. She served corned beef and jacket potatoes with corn on the cob. Marcos was ravenous but he waited for a sign from the others.

Come on, eat up now, the woman said.

Janice cut up her corned beef but just pushed it round her plate. Robert stuck his fork into the baked potato and left it there sticking up, like Excalibur.

If you eat up there's ice cream for dessert, she said.

Always in the same chirpy tone. It was unreal. Their mother had disappeared and she tried to jolly them along like they were on a camping holiday.

Where are you from? Robert said.

The woman looked startled at first, then pleased that someone was showing an interest.

I'm from Australia, from Adelaide to be more precise. That's a long way away.

She started prattling away about Australia, thinking she could strike up a relationship with him, but she didn't know Robert. He looked past her at the sideboard. She'd given him all the information he wanted; he wasn't interested in her. He dropped a pat of butter on the corn cob and another on the potato, picked up his plate and knife and fork and announced he was going to eat in his bedroom.

Now you sit down, young man. In this house we eat at the table, not in the bedroom.

We, he said to the back of her head as he left the room, plate in hand. Who's we?

Janice and Marcos waited to see what she would do. Would she try to force him to eat at the table? Robert was thirteen years old and he was as tall as her. But he was skinny and she was probably stronger, heavier certainly. But Robert's strength was in his will. If he didn't want to do something, no one could make him do it. He didn't care if he was punished. He'd take the punishment but he still wouldn't do it. Maybe the woman sensed this, or maybe she didn't want to pick a fight on her first day, so she just shook her head and tut-tutted and turned her attention to Marcos.

She leant across and picked up his knife and fork. She slit open the potato and lathered it with butter, then did the same with the corn. Her hair was nearly in his face and he could smell her. It wasn't a bad smell, it was just what women smelled like, talcum powder and hair spray, but he didn't like it. His stomach rumbled. He looked at Janice who was turning the corn cob in her hands but not eating it. On his plate the melted butter dribbled out each end of the potato and the aroma of buttery potato wafted up to him. The woman handed him the knife and fork. He looked at his plate, too ashamed to look at his sister, then cut off a chunk off butter-soaked potato and put it in his mouth. It tasted delicious but it felt like betrayal.

Later, lying in bed in the dark, he asked his brother if he'd eaten his dinner.

Yes, did you?

Yes.

It's OK, Marcos. We have to eat. Mum wouldn't want us to starve.

When he got home from school the following day the apartment smelled of bleach. Like a hospital, Marcos thought. Now the place was so spotlessly clean he could see how grubby it was before but he preferred it that way; it was unkempt but it was still his mother's house, now his mother was being eliminated, disinfected. The woman had moved things too. His mother's collection of small soapstone carvings of animals that she kept on the sideboard were now on a bookshelf.

She shouldn't do that, should she, Janice, he said. It's not for her to move mum's things.

Janice nodded.

I hate the fat cow, she said.

That evening their father came home for dinner. He sat at the head of the table, as always, and the woman Nancy sat opposite, which was their mother's place.

So how is everyone? he said in a cheery voice they'd never heard before, as though everything was completely normal. He wasn't the cheery type; he was stern and remote and they were all scared of him. Not that he was violent – he contracted out the corporal punishment to their mother – but because he was cold and never praised them or said anything positive about what they were doing, like when Janice showed him the badge she'd got for art in the Brownies and he just shrugged and gave a dismissive snort.

The woman had made beef stroganoff, which was a dish their mother cooked on special occasions. Was she trying to be their mother? Was she trying to replace her? She ladled the meat and sauce on to a plate which they passed along to their father, and then served the rest of them.

Hmm, this smells good, their father said, again in that fake, upbeat tone.

Marcos looked over to Robert to see if he'd rebel again and take his dinner to his room, but he stayed where he was, contemplating the plate of food like a chess player considering his next move.

Bon appetit, the woman said.

No one said anything and for several minutes there was just the sound of cutlery on china. Marcos ate but was so tense he found it hard to swallow and was afraid he might choke. When he did start to choke Janice smacked his back so hard a mushroom flew out of his mouth and on to the plate.

Marcos! Where are your manners? the Nancy woman said.

He glanced at his father in case he was going to tell the woman it wasn't for her to scold him but his father just looked past him as though he hadn't noticed or wasn't interested.

What's wrong with mum? Robert said. You could see he'd been working up the courage to ask.

She's not well, their father said, loading his fork with rice and not looking at anyone in particular.

What kind of not well?

It's complicated. Difficult to explain.

Did she have an accident?

No, nothing like that.

So she's got cancer.

Cancer? Who said she had cancer? Where did you get that idea from?

I don't know, it was just a guess.

Why can't you tell us? It was Janice asking now.

So many questions! Look, your mother is in good hands, and so are you, he added, nodding towards the Nancy woman. The three of them turned to look at her and she smiled.

Oh, don't you worry, you'll be well looked after, she said.

Is she in hospital? Marcos asked, the tears welling up in his throat.

I told you, she's in good hands, he said crossly, now finish your dinner and stop asking so many questions.

Robert looked first at Marcos, then Janice.

This is because of that lawyer, isn't it? he said. Because of what we said.

Their father banged his fist on the table, making the cutlery jump on their plates.

It's got nothing to do with that. I told you, your mother's not well, now just leave it at that.

But when is she coming back? Janice said. She was crying.

He raised his hand as though about to smack her, then pushed his chair back and left the room, slamming the door behind him.

Now look what you've done, the woman said to Janice. You go right now and tell your father you're sorry.

Janice got up and turned in the direction of her room. The woman stuck out a hand to stop her but Janice brushed it away.

Don't you touch me, she shrieked. Ever!

Robert and Marcos lay in their beds on opposite sides of the room. Robert was very territorial and made it clear where his side of the room began and Marcos' ended. He went nuts if his little brother encroached on his territory. Robert was reading a Hardy Boys adventure. Marcos felt very alone. His mother had disappeared and the only other people he could turn to, his brother and sister, were always at war with each other. Whatever they offered him, the nice things they said, the treats they promised, it was all just another ruse to win him over to their side of the argument. They each needed him as an ally, but that wasn't what he needed from them. He longed for a hug or a comforting arm around his shoulder but the only person offering comfort was the Nancy woman and he didn't want her consolation. To accept it would be to give in, to think the unthinkable, that his mother had gone and wasn't coming back.

Can I ask you something? Marcos said.

I'm reading.

Marcos looked up at the ceiling. He willed his brother to put his book down.

What? Robert said after a while.

Do you think mum's dead?

The tears welled up the moment he said the word dead.

I don't think so.

But you don't know so.

I don't know any more than you do, but I don't think so.

What then? Why won't dad tell us? Why is everyone being so secretive?

I don't know.

We have to find out, Marcos said, propping himself up on one elbow. It's a mystery and we have to solve it, he said, wiping his eyes.

Like the Hardy Boys, Robert laughed.

Yes, why not?

The Hardy Boys are stories. They're made up. We wouldn't know where to begin.

I do.

Where?

At the hospital.

Robert turned out the light but Marcos couldn't sleep. He lay in the dark trying to picture his mother the way she was before she did nothing but sit at the kitchen table and smoke, when she still had time for them, before they became an irritation, and when she still cooked beef stroganoff and lemon meringue pie. Back then, even when she scolded them, it was just a gentle scold, like the time she discovered he'd been hanging around the freight yards.

It was all because of the ice man. Maybe he was the last ice man on earth, before everyone got a refrigerator, but there he was, perched on the seat of a horse-drawn flatback cart. The vast block of ice, as big as a coffin, looked so out of place, unreal almost, like something that had fallen from the sky. When he told his mother, she asked where he'd seen him.

Just down the road, on rue Béthune.

As soon as he said it, he realised his mistake. To get to Béthune he had to cross rue Sainte-Catherine, which he wasn't allowed to on his own. His mother frowned.

On your own?

No, he lied, I was with Robert.

Are you telling the truth?

She said it in such a soft way he couldn't lie. If she'd been angry, if she threatened him with the strap, he would have maintained the lie to the bitter end but when she asked like that he couldn't, because what she was really asking was are you going to disappoint me and that was the last thing he wanted to do.

No, I was on my own, I'm sorry.

Well, don't do it again. It's a busy street, it's dangerous. What were you doing down there anyway?

He looked at her, her wide mouth and pointed chin, and he felt he could tell her anything and she would understand. And she did. She was always interested, always asked questions, never made him feel foolish.

I go to watch the trains.

There was a freight yard at the end of rue Béthune. Marcos would lean against the chain-link fence and watch for hours as the engines shunted the freight cars together, listening to the shudder of the cars as the couplings linked, the shriek of metal on metal, and sometimes in the distance the mournful horns of ships on the river. He persuaded Janice to go with him once but she got bored. Why would I want to look at trains all day? she said.

In class he wrote a short story about seeing the ice man, except in his story the horse bolted, tipping over the cart and the ice block shattered into a thousand pieces and the ice man stood with his hands on his head as the ice melted on the hot road. His teacher was Miss Hair, who was as enthusiastic and encouraging as she was stern. She would whack a child across the back of their head with a big wooden ruler if she thought they were daydreaming. Marcos liked her but he was also scared of her, everyone was. So when she asked him to stay behind after class, he wondered what he'd done wrong. As she gathered her books in her arms he urgently needed to pee. She led him to her office and a moment later they were joined by her sister, also only ever known as Miss Hair, who also taught at the school.

I liked your story about the ice man, his Miss Hair said. I liked it so much I showed it to my sister, who is an even keener reader than I and a good judge of writing.

It's a fine piece of writing, her sister said. Very well observed.

The two women exchanged glances. They weren't twins but were clearly sisters. They had the same grey eyes and wore their auburn hair in buns and both wore similar shirtwaist dresses and flat pumps. It took Marcos a moment to understand that he wasn't in trouble and, in fact, they'd singled him out for praise.

You have talent, his Miss Hair said. Have you ever thought about being a writer?

He had not. He was nine years old and if he'd pictured himself that far in the future it was driving the small locomotive that shunted the cars together in the freight yard, either that or the man who operated the wrecking ball. He spent an entire afternoon watching a factory being demolished, the operator swinging the crane away from the building and then swinging it back so the heavy ball smashed into the brickwork. It looked like the best fun in the world. Marcos shook his head.

Well, you should think about it, she said, and her sister nodded. Off you go then, dismissed.

That was the last time he saw the ice man.

When he met Janice after school the first thing she said was he couldn't go to the hospital on his own.

It's miles away. Besides, you're only nine, they won't tell you anything.

That's why you have to come with me.

I can't. I've got Brownies at five o'clock.

So, it's only half-past three. We have time. Come on, he said, pulling at the strap of her school bag.

Stop pulling me. I'm not going. I'll be late and then I won't get my badge.

What's more important, finding mum or your stupid badge?

It's not stupid and I'm not going. It's too far.

OK, I'll go by myself, he said and started walking up the hill away from her.

She either had to stop him or go with him. She was responsible for him. If she came home without him, she'd be the one in trouble, not him. Except she wouldn't be in trouble with mum because mum wasn't there and Marcos knew his sister didn't care what the Nancy woman said. It was a risk; she might just let him walk off on his own. He kept walking, but not too fast, and forced himself not to look back. A moment later she caught up with him.

Do you know how to get there? she said.

No, all I know is it's on Cedar Avenue. I looked it up in the phone book.

Cedar Avenue? OK, we can get a bus on The Boulevard.

The hospital was enormous. They stood in the entrance hall and looked at the signs.

Emergencies? Marcos said.

I don't think so. Let's try Admissions.

They stood in line at the admissions desk. The woman at the desk had brown bangs and glasses with cat's eye frames. She looked up the names of patients in a large register and then directed the visitors to the relevant part of the hospital.

This should be easy-peasy, Janice whispered.

When it was their turn the woman looked up over the top of her glasses and smiled. She did actually look a bit like a cat.

We're looking for our mother, Janice said. She was in a car accident.

Marcos was impressed. She sounded so convincing.

Oh dear, I'm sorry. And when did this happen?

This morning. Well, no, not this morning. It was three days ago. We only found out today. We were away when it happened. At camp.

At camp? In April? the woman said tonelessly.

Yes. With the Brownies.

With the Brownies. Both of you? she said, giving Marcos a half smile. Marcos looked down at his feet. Easy-peasy, Janice had said, but now she'd screwed up.

What's your mother's name?

Kaplan, Marion Kaplan.

The cat woman, turned the pages of the register and ran her finger down the left-hand column.

Another woman appeared behind the desk. They could tell she was a doctor because she wore a white coat and stethoscope around her neck. She smiled at them.

They're looking for their mother, the cat woman said, while continuing to check the list of names. They say she had an accident.

Oh really, oh I'm so sorry, but I'm sure she'll be all right.

Kaplan, the admissions woman said. I don't see anyone of that name.

Kaplan? The doctor said. There's a Dr Kaplan here. Peter Kaplan, is he your father by any chance?

Simultaneously Janice shook her head and Marcos nodded. The two women exchanged looks.

Perhaps I should call your father, the doctor said.

Janice tugged at her brother's shirt. It was all the signal he needed. They both turned and ran. On the way home they bumped into Janice's friend Arlene and another girl called Linda near the park. They wanted to know what was wrong.

What do you mean? There's nothing wrong.

But you look like you'd seen a ghost, you both do.

We've just been running, that's all. Sorry, we're in a bit of a rush. Bye.

She took Marcos' hand and they ran off again. Marcos understood that his sister hadn't told her friends about their mother. Nor had he and nor had either of them invited friends home since. They knew it was secret even if they didn't know why.

They spent the rest of the afternoon dreading their father coming home. They hadn't really done anything wrong. They were trying to find their mother. What could be wrong with that? But they knew they'd be in trouble. When they told Robert he said they were stupid and what did they expect.

Do you think a hospital is going to give out information about patients to a couple of kids? You have to be kidding. And what did you think you were doing taking Marcos with you?

It was his idea.

So what if it was his idea, you shouldn't have gone.

At least we did something, Janice spat back. What are you doing to find out what's happened to mum?

What do you want me to do?

You could have gone to the hospital, you're the oldest. Maybe they would have told you something.

Maybe she's not even in the hospital. Let's face it, we don't know anything. One day this woman arrives and dad says he's paying her to look after us. Then half the time he doesn't come home at night, so what do you think that means?

Maybe he's at work. You know, he's always working.

All night?

What then?

Go figure.

I don't get it.

Oh, please just go away. Get out of my room.

It's my room, too, Marcos piped up.

I don't care, just go away. Take your stupid sister and think up some other dumb plan.

But Marcos didn't follow his sister to her room. He sat on a chair in the living room and rocked back and forth, bouncy-wounce, bouncy-wounce. He was miserable. He missed his mother so much it hurt his chest. And all his brother and sister did was fight. Soon his father would come home and they'd be in hot water. Or maybe he wouldn't come home, maybe he'd go wherever he went when he didn't come home.

But he did come home and he went straight to his study until suppertime. Then at suppertime he didn't say anything, not about them going to the hospital, not about anything. No one spoke except the Nancy woman who was always prattling on about something. Then when she started clearing the plates their father said that in future they were all to come straight home from school, no dawdling, and no meddling in things that weren't their business. That was all. And then he left the house.

That night, while the Nancy woman was doing the dishes, Marcos tiptoed into his parents' bedroom and opened his mother's jewellery box. He took out a green and gold Wedgwood brooch and put it in his pocket. He slept with it under his pillow and in the morning hid it in a secret place. He started getting ready for school when his brother rolled over in bed.

What are you doing? he said in a cross sleepy voice. It's Saturday.

He hadn't realised, but he was dressed now so he went outside and sat on the stoop. The milkman from J.J. Joubert pulled a crate of milk from his truck.

One or two, today? He called out.

Marcos shrugged.

It's usually two on Saturday. Go on and check with your mother.

She's not here. She's gone to the supermarket.

The milkman gave him a look.

Everything OK, son?

Marcos shrugged again.

I guess, he said.

His best friends from school all had more money than his family and lived up the hill. At Christmas they all escaped the winter to spend a couple of weeks water-skiing in Florida. Marcos couldn't imagine his family doing fun things like water-skiing, even if they had the money. Even when they went on holiday his father was always working on some paper he had to deliver and they had to tiptoe round him, and his mother, when she wasn't cooking and cleaning, had her face in a book. They weren't a playful family. Marcos and Robert played ice hockey and Janice skied in winter, but just on Mont Royal, not like their friends who went to resorts in the Laurentians. The thing with his friends living up the hill meant they were on the other side of Sherbrooke, which he wasn't allowed to cross on his own, and if Janice wouldn't take him, he was stuck at home.

There was the boy next door, Tony, whose family were Italian, and they played cowboys sometimes round the back of the houses where some of the central heating boilers were mounted in clapboard shacks stuck on the back of the building which were a bit like something from a Wild West town like Tombstone. Marcos liked to play Paladin from *Have Gun Will Travel.* Tony's favourite was Maverick. Tony had a Remington rifle. Marcos carried a shiny Colt .45 in a black holster and a Derringer in his sock. Tony was fun to play with, but they weren't close.

Cigar smoke drifted up to where Marcos sat on the stoop. That was M. Lefebvre who lived in the basement apartment and seemed to spend most of his life on a chair by his front door smoking White Owl cigars in a yellow plastic holder. His teeth were the same shade of yellow. Marcos had said hello to him every day of his life but they'd never had a conversation. M. Lefebvre was French. Half the city was French but M. Lefebvre was, as far as he knew, the only French person living on their street. There were Italians, Greeks, Hungarians,

Russians and Scots, but no French. Nor were there any French kids at school. The French all lived somewhere else, in the old city or down by the river, his mother said, or maybe in Outremont.

Instead of waiting for Tony, Marcos took off in the direction of the freight yard. He waited at the end of his street for a gap in the traffic, then ran across Sainte-Catherine. He felt bad because it was like he was lying to his mother even though she would never know. But then, it seemed that no one cared about him anymore, so he could do whatever he liked.

The locomotive was shunting together a line of filthy tanker cars streaked with some sort of oil that in turn was caked with dirt. He was entranced by the harsh beauty of the yard, the steel rails and wooden boxcars, the clatter and screech of the locomotive's wheels, patient and purposeful as it assembled trains bound for who knows where. Once the tankers were coupled together on the siding, a big loco appeared and reversed into the line of cars. The driver, dressed in striped grey overalls, got out and checked the coupling.

Marcos heard a man's voice behind him. He turned to see a man in an old, greasy suit, with dishevelled hair and bright blue eyes.

That'll be heading up to Point-Aux-Trembles, he said, tilting his head in the direction of the train. To the refinery.

The man took a step closer. Marcos didn't move.

I see you hanging around here, the man said.

When he talked flecks of saliva gathered in the corners of his mouth. The man licked them away. The way he said hanging around made it sound like Marcos was doing something wrong.

I like watching the trains, he said, meaning he didn't see any harm in that.

I figured that. You live nearby?

Marcos nodded. The man scared him, though he didn't know why. He moved away from the fence.

I've got to go now.

Come on now, what's the rush? We could go and get a soda. Bet you'd like that.

The man took another step towards him.

Really, I'm late. My mum will kill me if I'm not back.

As he moved to go the man reached out and grabbed his wrist. Marcos slipped his grip and ran and didn't look back until he got to Sainte-Catherine. The man was where he'd left him, by the fence. He raised his arm by way of salute.

When Marcos got home he went round the back of the house to catch his breath. He was shaking all over. He was scared, but most of all he was scared that he'd get found out. It was all his fault, he should never have been there. He wanted to blurt it out and for someone to put an arm around him and say hush now it's alright, you're safe, for his mother to scold him in the gentle way she used to before she started spending her days at the kitchen table smoking. But he couldn't tell anyone, he was too scared and there was something about the creepy man that made him feel ashamed.

Time passed, a week, ten days, with no news of their mother. Janice asked why they couldn't visit her in hospital and the Nancy woman said the doctors said it was better if they didn't, she needed rest, she needed to be left in peace. Meanwhile, the Nancy woman continued her campaign to wear down their resistance and win them over. With Marcos it was food - chocolate chip cookies, strawberry ice cream, dill pickles – she had a nose for his favourite food and he was too weak or hungry to resist. He was in a growing spurt and was hungry all the time. But he fought off her attempts to cuddle him and wriggled out of her embrace whenever she tried. It wasn't just because giving in to her would be giving in to his mother being gone, there was something about her he found physically repulsive, nauseating almost; the ample and shapeless softness of her and her peculiar, cloying smell, not really a perfume smell, more like air freshener.

With Janice she played the we girls have got to stick together card which, with two brothers, one of whom she'd fought with almost from birth, was a chink in Janice's armour. Also, Janice was twelve and on the threshold of the age of total confusion, she needed the solace and solidarity of female company. But she, like Marcos, was repelled by the Nancy woman and fended her off. Then one evening when Janice sat at the table doing her homework, the woman came up behind her and started brushing her hair. She resisted at first but her hair was full of tats and she gave in, though with little grace, the way a cat lets you stroke it as though it were doing you a favour.

The Nancy woman's biggest challenge was Robert. After that first day, when he defiantly took his dinner to his bedroom, he changed tack. He was impeccably polite. Whatever she asked him to do, he did it. Whatever food she produced, he ate it. If she asked him to wash the dishes, he didn't argue with her, he didn't say it's not my turn, he did it. He complied, silently, with neither a word of complaint nor of thanks. But it was a parody of compliance. He became the embodiment of insubordinate contempt, turning obedience into defiance, with both her and his father. There was nothing they could do; they commanded and he obeyed, like a robot or a zombie; what more could they ask of him? Meanwhile, he continued to withdraw into himself, and barely spoke to anyone. In bed at night, if Marcos asked him a question, he either wouldn't answer or only after he'd asked the same question three or four times. And even then, all he got was a yes or a no or an I don't know.

As for Janice, she gradually began to transfer her resentment of the Nancy woman towards her mother. She felt abandoned – they all did – and Janice started to interpret her mother's disappearance, or desertion, as somehow directed at her, something intended to wound or even to punish her. And, as she saw no grounds for this punishment, that it was undeserved, her resentment and sense of injustice grew every day her mother was away. Not that she warmed to the Nancy woman whom she habitually referred to as that fat cow or that fat, smelly cow. Why has mum done this to us? she said. Why doesn't she come back? It's not fair, she told Marcos. It's just not fair.

Marcos now spent several hours a day, in fact, most of the time that he was at home, rocking back and forth in the same armchair, mouthing his bouncy-wounce mantra. Everyone else had ceased to notice, or were so accustomed to it that they'd stopped telling him off, apart from his father, but he was rarely home. He stopped when his father told him to, but resumed soon after, miming the bouncy-wounce words, soundlessly moving his lips. It was a comfort, the rhythmic motion, but it also served as a refusal to accept things as they were, a way of not thinking at all. Above all, it was an incantation, a monotonous prayer; he was calling on his mother to return.

He admired his brother's aloof disdain but it wasn't something Marcos felt able to emulate. He was too young and too needy. His brother was thirteen, he existed on another level and had other imperatives. In their different ways, Robert and Janice had shut themselves away behind a barricade of hurt and indignation and were of little help to Marcos. As for his father, he had never fulfilled the love function, nor was he expected to. Fathers worked. They put food on the table and laid down the law. It was understood that they were not to be trifled with skinned knees, fickle school friends or problems in the classroom and the playground. Anything that came under the heading Love was a mother's domain.

But now Marcos had no mother and had trouble in the classroom and the playground. The same Miss Hair who had praised his essay on the ice man had in the past week twice whacked him with the wooden ruler, once for daydreaming and the second time for forgetting his homework. (He hadn't forgotten it; he simply didn't bother to do it.) What was worse, he had become the target of a well-known bully named Bruce from the year above him and who happened to live on Grosvenor, Marcos' street. Marcos had no idea why he'd been singled out; perhaps Bruce had a nose for vulnerability. He bullied him in the playground and threatened to beat him up if he showed his face on the street. My street, he said, like no one else lived there. Bruce was only ten but he was bigger than Marcos and, like most bullies, he had his camp followers who would happily beat Marcos up in order to win his approval.

Marcos wasn't in a position to be aloof, and anyway lacked his brother's gift of masking his emotions. What he needed above all was comfort, to be wrapped in his mother's arms, in her lavender and tobacco embrace, and be told that everything was alright. He rebuffed the Nancy woman's attempts to embrace him and also avoided calling her by her name.

But it was only a matter of time. One afternoon after school he was rocking back and forth when she told him to stop. When he didn't, she put her hands on his shoulders and forced him to stop. He sat, motionless and rigid. She slowly released her grip and then sat down beside him. There wasn't room for two and he was wedged between her and the arm of the chair. She put an arm round his shoulder. There was nothing he could do: he was stuck there.

You know why you're not allowed to visit your mother in hospital, don't you?

He didn't. He had no idea. He shook his head.

She's not in a normal hospital, not the sort of hospital you go to when you break a leg or need an operation.

Marcos looked at her sidelong.

She tapped the side of her head, widening her eyes as she did so.

She's not right in the head, she said, tapping her temple once more. That's why she's been put away. Not right, do you understand?

He did. That is, he understood the words. But it was like when the lawyer asked who they'd rather live with, it didn't make sense. It didn't make sense that his mother wasn't right in the head, which meant she was mad. She wasn't. Who said she was mad? Just because she'd stopped cleaning and sat in the kitchen chain-smoking Export A? Did that qualify as mad? Did the others know, Robert and Janice? And if they did, why hadn't they told him? Why did he have to hear it from her? And if they didn't know, should he tell them? He was the baby; would they even believe him? It was as though a hole had opened up inside him and he'd fallen into it. He felt desperately alone, forsaken, abandoned.

Little by little she pulled him towards her, until his head rested on her shoulder and he was enveloped in her scent of hyacinths and bleach. She stroked his head and as he started to cry – he'd never cried in front of her before – she pulled him closer into her large softness and he didn't resist, he surrendered, even though he hated her almost as much as he hated himself for giving in, for needing her and letting her give him comfort. He felt weak and ashamed but he allowed her to enfold him in her pale freckled arms until he heard a key in the door, which was certain to be Janice, and he leapt out of her embrace and ran to his room before his sister could see him there in the Nancy woman's arms.

She says mum isn't in a normal hospital, he said to Janice later when they were out on the stoop, chewing spiral sticks of red liquorice.

Who said?

You know. Her.

What did she mean?

I think she means she's in a place for mad people.

What does she know? Stupid, fat cow.

Do you think mum has gone mad?

Don't be silly. Why would she? You shouldn't listen to that woman. She's evil.

After supper the Nancy woman caught hold of his arm and tried to give him a goodnight kiss but he twisted away.

Is it true mum is in a hospital for mad people? Marcos asked his brother after he switched the light off. Sometimes it was easier to talk in the dark.

Who told you that?

Who do you think?

Robert didn't answer. The darkness thrummed with his silence.

So it's true.

The bed creaked as Robert turned on his side but the darkness was now so dense the sound barely carried.

I thought you knew, he said.

It was Saturday again. Marcos scanned the street to see if the bully Bruce was in sight. As long as he was with

Janice, Bruce left him alone but sometimes on the way to school in the morning she abandoned him to go off with her friends once they'd crossed Sherbrooke, even though she was supposed to stay with him all the way past Westmount Avenue. Marcos lived in fear that Bruce would catch him when he was alone.

But Bruce was nowhere to be seen. Marcos knew M. Lefebvre was out by the waft of his White Owl cigar. Across the street his friend Tony's dad had his head under the hood of his yellow Buick Roadmaster. He had a set of new spark plugs lined up on the fender. The short spring was over and summer was just around the corner; he could tell from the sky, the height of it as much as anything else. Marcos usually looked forward to summer, all that time off school, but now there was the Nancy woman in the house and probably no holiday to look forward to, just going to the park, going to the pool, going downtown with Janice to walk around the department stores. And since that man tried to grab him, he was afraid to go back to the freight yard.

His friend Tommy had invited him to spend the day at his house. Tommy's family were rich. They lived on Summit Circle and always went to Florida in winter. But he told Tommy he couldn't go.

My mum won't let me, he lied.

But why?

I don't know. To tell you the truth, lately she's been a bit of a pain in the ass.

Why did he say that? For a moment when he said it, he felt defiant, strong, but then he felt ashamed. He'd started lying more of late or, if not actually lying, not truthing, about his mother. He hadn't mentioned it to anyone; no one told him not to, but he guessed he wasn't supposed to say anything. He thought about the last time he saw his mother. It was just like any other school morning. She kissed him and gave him a hug, same as always, though maybe she hugged him a little longer than usual. Maybe she knew she was going away. Everyone knows more than I do, he thought. His father must know but he didn't tell them anything. Besides he was hardly ever home, not even at night. Your father's work is very important, the Nancy woman said more than once. You can only hope to grow up to be half the man your father is.

Marcos wore his favourite green and white T-shirt with the boat neck collar that his mother had bought him last summer in Burlington, Vermont. In his left hand he held the yellow dumper truck that had real hydraulics so you could raise the back up slowly and watch the earth and stones slide out. In his right, the black Ford pickup. They were his two favourites. Between the path to his building and the one next door there was a stretch of dirt with a few tufts of grass. He knelt down, parked the pickup and drove the dumper truck through the dirt, pushing down so that it left tyre marks. Then he lay on his side so that he was at eye level with the truck. He gave the driver orders of what dirt to move where and each time the driver answered: You got it. Marcos made the sound of the big diesel engine and the sound of the hydraulics as he slowly raised the back and dumped out the earth. The rest of the world, the street and his family all faded into the distance. There was just him, the concrete warm against his body, his nails black with dirt, loading earth and pebbles into the truck, then dumping them out again. If Tony came and wanted to play, he'd tell him no, he'd rather play by himself, it was better that way, he could live in his imagination and didn't have to make room for anyone else. The way things stood, it looked like his mother was never coming back and he figured if he was going to be alone from now on, he better get good at it.

Ladies' Man

Men in general didn't like David for the simple reason that women in general did. He had something that clicked with women and it vexed men that they couldn't see what it was. He wasn't tall or rich nor, by any conventional yardstick, good looking. It was a mystery what drew women into his orbit, and yet they whirred around him like stray electrons.

He was also available, having separated from Luisa, mother of six-year-old Samuel, for whom David waited in the playground, chatting to two women, Raquel and Paula. They were both smiling, both in their late thirties, women watching their youth slip away. Recently emerged from the tunnel of sleeplessness and babies and nappies, they had arrived at an is that all there is moment in their lives. David had the knack of making them feel it wasn't, that there was more to come. They didn't have to *do* anything about it; they just needed to believe, but he put the emphasis on the word *do* and let it hang there as an option.

The parents lined up inside the walled playground that doubled as a basketball court. A tall, slender palm tree stood in one corner. It was an inner-city school and the parents were a mixed bunch - Latinos, Pakistanis, Moroccans and various Europeans as well as locals. There were two or three adopted children in each class, mostly Chinese and African.

Xavi and Rafa, also waiting for their kids, eyed David across the playground.

Whenever I see him, he's with a woman and the woman is laughing, Xavi said. What is that? Does he tell jokes?

It was the laughing that got to him, and the way they laughed: intimate, conspiratorial, flirtatious. Even his wife Laura; she didn't laugh like that at home.

The kids came out. David's son leapt into his arms like his dad was a returning war hero.

Raquel's taking you to the park with the twins, he said. I have to go to a meeting. I'll pick you up in an hour.

Xavi's son Pol ran out and at the same moment his wife Laura appeared at the gate. Pol hugged his mother's legs.

Wasn't I supposed to pick him up today? Xavi said.

Yes, I'm here for the meeting.

What meeting?

Parents association. Have you been drinking?

Drinking?

Yes, you smell of alcohol.

I had a glass of wine with lunch.

Laura shrugged. Xavi smelled of cognac, not wine. David came over.

Hey Laura, coming to the meeting? he said.

Sure. Catch you later, Xavi.

At the parents' association meeting Laura sat next to David along with half a dozen other parents arranged in a circle on the children's tiny green plywood chairs. The business of the meeting was organising the children's end of year excursion. It was a hot afternoon in late May. David was in shorts and Laura in a loose sundress. Laura could see why women were attracted to David with his easy-going manner. He was amusing and, for a man, refreshingly willing to make fun of himself. Even so, she'd never felt drawn to him. Or not until now.

Laura's eyes wandered over the childish paintings on the walls and her mind wandered to thoughts of David. One of the mothers was telling a long story that had nothing to do with the business in hand, something to do with her mother and hospital waiting lists. People used the meetings to sound off. Occasionally someone, often Laura herself, would say something like, could we stick to the agenda, please, which earned her dirty looks, as though it were rude not to let people waffle on about whatever entered their head.

Perhaps it was the boredom and knowing they'd just go round and round and not resolve anything, or perhaps it was the heat, but Laura became intensely aware of David at her side, the bare skin of his arms and legs seemed to be calling to her own bare skin in a force field of desire that drew their bodies closer together although neither of them moved. It seemed to come from nowhere, this sudden hunger, a desire that demanded appeasement. She looked sidelong at David who returned the look with a smile of recognition that said, yes, I feel it too. Or was that just her imagination?

Mayra, the president, was pushing for an outing to a picnic area in Arbúcies. Montse, her predecessor, whom Mayra had deposed in a crudely engineered coup, argued that instead of hiring buses they should just take the kids to the beach or to the park like they did every year.

There are deer at Arbúcies, and a river, Mayra said, as though that clinched it.

It's a two-hour journey, Montse said. The kids will get hungry, they'll be full of sugar, they'll go crazy. Total nightmare.

The next ten minutes was taken up by Edwin, a Dutchman who was driven by a constant need to demonstrate how politically correct he was. He was arguing that they needed to do more to get the Moroccan mothers to come on outings.

Perhaps someone could talk to Mina, Edwin said. She seems a bit more open, then maybe she could persuade some of the others. We really need to try to be more inclusive.

Mina's not Moroccan, Laura sighed. She's from Pakistan. But whatever.

David chuckled and gave her a conspiratorial nudge with his knee. Laura felt a shock of excitement at his touch. The meeting ended, as usual, without reaching a decision.

That Edwin gets on my nerves, Laura said on the way to the park to collect their children. He's so transparent. I mean really, does he think we don't see through all that I'm such a feminist man bollocks?

You'd rather he was a mainstream macho man?

There's got to be something in between. He tries too hard.

Xavi was in the park, rolling a cigarette in the shade of an acacia. Laura felt conscious of the sudden intimacy that had sprung up between her and David and, anxious that it might show, peeled away from him to join her friend Mariona. David joined his son and some other kids who were kicking a ball around in the dirt.

The two women sat on a bench by the swings. Mariona absent-mindedly rocked her new baby to sleep in its pushchair. Four Dominican men sat on upturned beer crates playing dominoes on a makeshift table. Young Moroccan kids with elaborate hair styles hung out, listening to scratchy reggaeton on a phone, waiting around for something to happen. The parrots screeched in the laburnums.

Is Xavi alright? Mariona asked.

Laura and Mariona had been friends since primary school. They discussed their partners the same way they talked about their children, as a set of behaviours to be navigated and, where possible, modified.

Alright how?

It was hot and Laura pushed her hair away from her face. She had lush, dark brown hair and every year when summer came around she thought about cutting it short, and then had second thoughts.

All I did was ask how work was going but he practically bit my head off.

Mariona had known Xavi even longer than Laura. The two met through her.

Don't take it personally. He's been very grumpy of

late. I don't know why. I worry he's turning into his father, one of those grumpy old men, you know the kind, talks out of his hat with such great authority. According to his father, everything is a con. Whatever the subject is, it could be the government or bus drivers' strike or the price of fish, the explanation's always the same, it's a scam, they're a mafia. Xavi's not that bad yet but I'm worried he's headed in that direction. He's a bit stuck. He hates his job, he doesn't get on with most of the people he works with. The trouble is, I can't talk to him about anything. I try but he just shuts me down. You know how he is, he's never been much of a talker, and definitely not someone who's prepared to discuss his problems.

Tell me about it, Mariona said. Rafa's the same. He acts like it's a personal attack when I ask how he's feeling. Like trying to talk something through is an admission of failure.

Xavi never wants to have sex. Says he's too tired. That's supposed to be our line, isn't it?

She looked over at David, recalling the touch of his knee at the meeting.

Sex, Mariona laughed, rocking the pushchair. Wow! That's the last thing on my mind. What I fantasise about is sleep. And I'm so fat now, who'd want to fuck me anyway? I never got this fat with the first two.

You'll lose it soon enough, you always do, Laura said, though she suspected that this time Mariona wouldn't bother.

The police were checking the Moroccan kids' ID. They made the boys empty their pockets. They complied with sullen obedience. They'd been through this dozens of times and, besides, their pockets were always empty.

I suppose you get what you pay for, Laura said.

What's that supposed to mean?

I mean I knew what I was getting into with Xavi. I was playing it safe. All those years when I was wild. You remember?

Sure. I used to worry about you.

Ha! I used to worry about me. I was trying to scare myself, see how far I dared to go. It worked, I got scared and I chose Xavi, a safe pair of hands.

He's a good guy, Laura. And a good father. Don't knock it.

Absolutely. And he was handsome when he still had his hair and before he started drinking at lunchtime. The point is, he isn't exciting; he never was. I was never excited by him. In a weird way, that was part of his attraction.

How do you mean?

Like I said, a safe bet. Steady, reliable, nothing unexpected. No surprises. The opposite of wild.

Yeah, well, I was never wild like you, but the way I see it, the exciting guys are for excitement but they're no good for the long haul and definitely not if you want to have babies. Especially not if you want your babies to have a father who sticks around. Like David over there.

What about him? Laura said, trying not to sound defensive.

He's exciting. Let's face it, he's definitely got something. But men like that should come with a warning:

Not suitable for long-term use or This product may seriously undermine your self-esteem.

You think?

I'm not saying he's bad. He's a good dad and he's funny, which is such a relief in a man. They all take themselves so seriously. But he's basically a gourmand and we women are his delicatessen.

Except he does actually seem to like women.

I'm sure he does in his gourmandish way. Fine, if you see yourself as an amuse bouche but don't expect him to hang around after dessert.

The cops got back in their car but didn't leave. The Moroccan boys went back to hanging out, acting like the cops weren't there, but watchful too.

The guys I used to go with back then …

The exciting guys?

Yeah, them. I wanted to have fun. I wanted to *be* fun. I thought we could have fun together. Of course, I liked that they fancied me. I wanted to feel wanted, loved. But there was something wrong, something they saw in me.

Wrong? Like how?

I don't know what it was, or is. Something I give off that men pick up on and that I bring out in them, something ugly. I think back to those times and those guys I went out with. I was too young to see it then but they didn't really like me – or most of them didn't. They liked that I was fun, a real good time girl, that I could drink as much as they did and that I didn't think fucking was such a big deal. But they didn't see me as their equal, I can see that now.

Laura looked over at David. She wondered if she slept with him if it would be like with the other guys and she'd end up feeling used. She realised she was willing to risk that disappointment.

So tell me, Xavi asked Laura when they got home. What is it about David? What's the big attraction?

Xavi leaned against the door frame. The lunchtime drink was wearing off and he was feeling edgy. If he could just sink a can he'd get some of his buoyancy back. Laura was folding the washing. It startled her that her husband should mention David like that, out of the blue. Since the school meeting she hadn't been able to get him out of her mind. Could Xavi tell what she was thinking? Could he read her mind? She didn't look up lest her face gave her away.

What big attraction do you mean?

Why do all you women find him so irresistible? You all buzz around him like flies around shit.

Like flies round shit, what a charming image. And what's that supposed to mean, all you women? I don't think all women think he's so attractive. I don't, for a start.

Don't you? OK, let's say you don't. But lots of women do. He's always surrounded by them.

Are you jealous?

Not jealous. Curious.

You sound jealous.

Their son Pol came into the kitchen, demanding a sandwich. Laura looked at Xavi but he didn't move from the doorway. The child pulled impatiently at her dress.

Just a moment, Pol, Laura said, and then said to Xavi, over the child's head, maybe it's because he's not afraid to seem vulnerable. You men are so shit scared that anyone will think you're weak, but David doesn't seem to care. I imagine some women would find that attractive.

So, is that it? You all want to mother him?

Laura sighed.

Frankly, some of us have had a gutful of mothering, she said. Daddy will make you a sandwich, Pol, she told her son as she pushed past Xavi out of the kitchen.

David sat on his bike at an intersection, waiting for the lights to change. A young woman with chestnut hair crossed in front of him. The reddish-brown of her hair, redolent of candlelight and firesides, fell against the burgundy red of her shirt and contrasted with the darker brown of her eyebrows and the rose-white pallor of her skin. She felt his eyes on her and they exchanged glances, the non-committal urban glance that in a second suggests and dismisses myriad possibilities. As she reached the pavement on the other side he willed her to look back. The lights changed. A car behind him beeped. He waited a second longer. The car swerved round him and the driver shouted something. The woman with the chestnut hair turned, he smiled, she smiled back and then he rode off and it was over, forgotten.

Laura didn't consciously decide to sleep with David, she simply created the circumstances that made it possible and therefore likely to happen. Knowing that David had once been an electrician, all Laura did was mention how annoying it was that a dimmer switch that they'd installed barely a year ago had started flickering. That was David's cue to volunteer to take a look at the problem.

Will there be a call-out charge? she asked with unintended flirtatiousness. David smiled.

There usually is, but I guess I could waive it in the circumstances, us being friends and all. When would suit you? I'm free tomorrow morning, if that works for you.

That would be great, she said. She had a sensation of leaping into the dark.

The next morning she called work to say she had a doctor's appointment and would be in late. David arrived. He followed her down the hall, carrying his tool bag. He was dressed the same as her, in cut-off jeans and a white T-shirt.

We could be twins, he said. Laura laughed and turned away as she felt herself starting to blush.

He'd never been in her apartment before. He scanned the furniture, the pictures on the wall, the books and the discarded toys. The inside of someone's home is like a peek backstage into their life; it tells you things that don't show on the outside, quite often unexpected things, such as Laura's taste in floral furnishings. David wouldn't have predicted that. Laura was conscious of him being in her home and that it was right here, the home she shared with Xavi, that she was going to cheat on her husband. The thought provoked a frisson of equal parts guilt and excitement. David, too, was excited, like an intruder who is about to burgle a house. He sensed in

Laura that clash of raw hunger and timidity of a woman who hasn't been with anyone but her husband for years.

He twiddled the dimmer switch on and off and, just as she said, it flickered when turned down low.

If you're lucky, it's the bulb that's the problem, not the switch. Switches are expensive.

He stood on a chair, reached up and unscrewed the bulb. His T-shirt rode up.

You're in luck, he said, getting down from the chair. It's the bulb. This is a LED light but not a dimmable one.

You just need to replace the bulb with one that dims. It's a special type. Look.

Laura came and stood beside him.

See, it's a LED light but it should say dimmable and it has a symbol, a sort of squiggle like the recycling symbol. Change the bulb and your troubles will be over.

She bent her head to look at the light bulb in his hand. He studied her pale neck. He was pretty sure what was going to happen next but he waited for a sign from her. She, too, was waiting for a sign, but then made the move herself. She touched her bare arm against his. That was enough. David took it from there.

By the time the end of year school excursion came around, the affair was several weeks old. It consisted almost entirely of furtive, often hurried, but nevertheless thrilling and deeply satisfying sex, sometimes in her bed, sometimes his, sometimes they didn't get as far as a bed. Mariona said men like David should come with a warning that they will seriously damage your self-esteem but in the warmth of David's embrace Laura's self-esteem rose like bread in the oven.

Over those few weeks they – or rather she – became increasingly reckless. With each new tryst she extended the margin of risk. On one occasion Xavi came home early and missed catching David in his bed by a matter of minutes. Laura was risking everything and was terrified of being found out but the risk added to the excitement. She needn't have worried about David. He was a pro and a master of discretion but infatuation incited Laura to shout it from the rooftops, He's my man! Except of course David was no one's man but his own. That's what baffled men like Xavi: women could see what he was but, rather than run a mile, they gathered round.

To begin with, all she wanted was a little adventure, a one-off, a day trip away from her life with Xavi, a little fuck you to normality. But it hadn't worked out that way; she wanted more. At the start she saw David as a recreational drug that she imagined would have worn off by now, but it hadn't. David was like smoking crack; he left her aching for more. And David didn't make her feel like those other guys, like she was just a ride they took for a while. He was an affectionate, attentive lover. He made her feel, if not loved, then loveable. It was confusing.

There was no denying it, she enjoyed the deceit, the getting away with it one more time, the close shaves, the clandestinity, the hastily concocted excuses and alibis. living a double life.

But she felt bad, too, and oscillated between guilt and resentment towards Xavi. Xavi didn't deserve this. If she was bored that was her choice and her fault. She was angry with herself for the choices she'd made, lazy, safe choices, like sitting the civil service exam so as to land a well-paid but meaningless job for life. Xavi had done the same. Their jobs were unnecessary; it would make no difference to anyone if they never went in to work. It was unfair to take that out on Xavi. He hadn't done anything wrong; he was who he was. Since she'd been seeing David, Xavi couldn't put a foot right. Laura constantly had to suppress her irritation. Everything he did annoyed her: the way he ate, his gestures, his opinions, even the sound of his voice.

Perhaps sensing something was up he arranged a babysitter then took Laura out for a surprise dinner at her favourite Japanese restaurant. She put on a good face but the conversation was forced, sporadic and punctuated by uneasy silences. When he asked her if anything was wrong, she said no, she was just tired, and then later when he asked her for a second time she snapped at him and the evening ended badly.

As for David, what was he thinking? She had no idea. It no longer felt like a fling. He continued to be assiduously loving and affectionate. He flattered her. He told her she was beautiful and made her feel that she was. Men say things like, you've got beautiful eyes or lovely hair but that's before they get you into bed. Afterwards they never mention your hair or your eyes again. But not David. He worshipped at the temple of her body, all of it. He even said he liked her nose, which she thought was her worst feature. It was too long, like her face.

But was there love behind all this loving or was it like Mariona said, that David was a gourmet and Laura just another fine spread? Did it matter? If David declared his love for her, she would probably freak out. That took things to another level. It implied choosing between him and Xavi. That was never part of the plan.

And yet the uncertainty nagged at her. David talked with his hands and his lips and his cock but he didn't let on how he was feeling. He was there to enjoy and to be enjoyed. He made that plain, without saying as much. He wasn't about to rescue her from a dull marriage. On the contrary, she imagined it suited him perfectly that she was married and therefore had no business demanding more of him. And yet he made her feel – or at least, let her imagine – that there could be more, that he really cared for her.

I wish we could spend a whole night together, just one night, or a weekend, she said one afternoon in his bed. A weekend in a hotel by the sea. Wouldn't that be great?

Um-hum, he said, stroking her hair.

He didn't say, yes, that would be brilliant. Um-hum was all he said. She didn't push him for more. Ambiguity was David's preferred terrain. Laura felt she didn't have any call on him. She'd started it, after all.

Time passed, they continued the affair without getting caught. Then two weeks before the summer break the children came home with a note in their school bags explaining that they were going to Arbúcies for the end of year excursion. To cover costs, parents had to pay €15 per child, some of which would go towards subsidising less well-to-do families. This hadn't been decided at any meeting, it was an executive decision by Mayra, determined to show her predecessor Montse who was boss. In the playground Montse and her supporters muttered about insurrection but everyone knew it was too late to organise anything else. It was a fait accompli.

Xavi, who usually tried to opt out of school events, announced that he was going. Mariona said she couldn't face all that driving with the baby and Laura agreed to take Rafa, the eldest of her three. On the bus, Xavi sat with Karim, a soft-spoken Moroccan who was with his children Omar and Nadia. As expected, none of the Moroccan mothers showed up. Laura sat with Núria, who had recently separated from her partner.

After an hour the children started to complain. When were they going to get there? How much longer? I'm hungry. Parents started muttering too. Whose idea was it to go somewhere so far away?

Ask Mayra, Montse said primly. It was her decision.

But no one asked Mayra. Instead they pacified the restive children with crisps and sweets and chocolate with entirely foreseeable consequences. There was an accident somewhere up ahead and the traffic slowed to a crawl and then a standstill. Children started running up and down the aisle. There were fights and shouting. It was chaos. One little boy was sick. That set off a few more until the bus reeked of vomit. By the time they arrived, nearly three hours later, half the picnic had been eaten.

There were half a dozen picnic tables on the edge of a small woodland and beyond that a shallow, fast-flowing creek. There was no sign of the promised deer. Instead, a group of shirtless men were playing football on a dusty pitch. There was something sinister and hostile about the men; everyone felt it. They eyed up the women as they unloaded the food on to the tables while the children ran around shrieking. They waved some of the kids over to join them but the kids held back instinctively.

Some of the men came over and started hanging around in a vaguely threatening way. Everyone went about their business, pretending they weren't there.

Where you come from? One of them asked in heavily-accented English.

People looked around, waiting for someone to respond. In the end it was David who spoke.

We're from Barcelona. We're on a school trip. How about you?

What?

Where are you from?

It was tense though no one could understand why. They'd just got off the bus and here they were in some sort of standoff with complete strangers.

From Belarus, the man said. Sailors.

They say they're sailors, David translated for the others.

They don't look like sailors, someone muttered in Catalan, assuming they wouldn't understand. They look like gangsters.

You're a long way from the sea, David said.

The man took a step towards him.

Just saying, David said.

One of the others called to the sailor-gangsters and they went back to kicking a ball around, all the time casting hostile glances towards the school group.

Montse held up her phone with a map of Belarus.

It's landlocked. So how can they be sailors? Working out well so far, she called in Mayra's direction, loud enough for everyone to hear. If we don't get raped or murdered it should be a fabulous day.

Beer, anyone? one of the dads asked, slapping a 12-pack on the table. Hurry up while they're still half-way cold.

Mayra frowned. She had specified that no one should bring alcohol because it would alienate the Muslims. Karim, the only Muslim present, accepted the offer of an Estrella. Núria produced a bottle of Ron Pujol and a litre of Coke.

Cubata, anyone?, she said. No ice, I'm afraid.

Mayra banged a Tupperware box on the table in anger and stalked off. The others looked askance. Núria poured a cubata and raised the paper cup in an ironic salute to Mayra's retreating back.

The Belarussian sailors took themselves off to the river and a football match was improvised among the children and parents. Someone had a frisbee, someone else beach tennis. The adults sat in the shade drinking beer (several other parents had ignored Mayra and brought supplies). They ate what was left of the lunch. It was too hot in the sun and the kids sat in the shade, playing with their phones, while the adults dozed. Xavi was asleep in the deep shade of a holm oak.

Laura had made a point of avoiding David up till then. She caught his eye and tilted her head in a gesture that said, follow me. She took the path that led up the hill into the woods. A few minutes later David followed. She leaned against a tree. They kissed.

I want to do it right here, she said.

It's too risky. Someone might come.

They're all asleep.

Not all of them.

I don't care. I really don't.

She slid her hand inside his shorts.

I want you. Now. Right here.

The bark chafed her skin. When she started moaning David put a hand over her mouth.

She was pulling her shorts up when they heard shouting from below and then people calling her name.

Jesus! What do they want?

You go, David said. I'll come a bit later so they don't suspect anything.

Laura straightened up her clothes and hurried down the path.

Where were you? Xavi said.

Nowhere, I went for a walk. What's up?

It's Rafa, he's gone missing.

Rafa? Mariona's Rafa?

But there wasn't any other Rafa in their party.

Missing? How?

Pol went looking for him to play frisbee but he's disappeared.

But he can't have disappeared. Where could he go?

Laura felt sick, a deep churning nausea, a toxic cocktail of dread and guilt. They divided into three groups to search the woods, the riverside and the area near the toilet block where the coach was parked. David meanwhile had appeared, though not by the path Laura had taken, and joined the search of the woods while Laura and Xavi and four others set off for the river. When they got there the Belarussian sailors were sitting on stones in the water in their underpants drinking beer.

Have you seen a boy? Laura asked in English. Small boy?

She held her palm out flat at around Rafa's height. One of the sailors leered and waved her over.

Come, come in water. Is good. Nice and cool. We have beer.

Laura ignored him and moved along the riverbank. She was close to tears. She'd never understood that expression about having your heart in your mouth till then, but there it was. She was practically choking on it. She silently vowed that she would abandon her affair with David, she would be a good and faithful wife, she would be good in every conceivable way if only Rafa was safe and sound.

An outcrop of rock blocked their path beside the river so they circled back towards the picnic tables just as the second group emerged from the woods. No sign of Rafa. Laura started to cry. We have to find him, don't just stand around talking, she wailed. Montse put an arm around her.

It's not your fault, Laura. I'm sure he's fine, he's probably just wandered off, the way boys do.

Laura slumped at the picnic table with her head in her hands. Núria, who was quite drunk, slid a paper cup of rum across the table.

Sorry, no Coke left. You'll have to drink it straight. You just sit for a moment, we'll find him.

And then, just as if nothing had happened, there was Rafa, looking bemused as everyone rushed towards him.

Where were you? We've been looking all over.

Up there, he said, pointing to a tree on the edge of the woods. I climbed up.

Didn't you hear us calling your name? We've been worried sick.

Rafa shrugged. Laura held out her open arms.

What's up, Laura? Why are you crying?

It's alright, Rafa. We were worried, that's all.

She put an arm round him and kissed the top of his head. Someone laid a comforting hand on her shoulder. It was Xavi.

It's alright, Laura. He's safe. Everything's OK.

She leaned her tear-streaked cheek on his hand.

As they lined up to get back on the bus David gave her arm a comforting squeeze. Laura pulled her arm away, not sharply, from the outside you'd hardly have noticed, but the message was clear: don't touch me. On the bus home she sat next to Xavi, watching the countryside peel by, then fell asleep with her head on his shoulder.

David sat at the back of the bus with Raquel whose twins were asleep on the seat beside her. David was telling her a story. Raquel was laughing.

Ima

Those pipe runs don't look right, Ima said in a low voice so the builder wouldn't hear. No way that's a one in twenty fall.

Phil nodded, not necessarily in agreement. As the architect, he had his professional amour propre to nurture, while she was, as she put it with her penchant for self-deprecation, merely an architect manqué. But she'd done her homework and knew her stuff and if she looked at a pipe run and said it wasn't one in twenty, she was probably right.

Ima wondered if he'd take the builder up on it. Knowing Phil, he'd say nothing then send the builder a terse text message telling him to put it right. Phil wasn't great at face to face, just as he wasn't great as a boyfriend, if that's what he was. Good enough in bed but not really up to scratch on the tender loving care front. But then nor was she if, she was honest. Sentimentality didn't fit with the arch and witty persona she'd so carefully constructed.

The builder said he needed to talk to Phil about something, implicitly excluding Ima. Builders couldn't make her out. It didn't add up that this chic woman with the posh accent should know about pipe falls or the U-value of dry linings. Ima didn't mind. If people found her enigmatic, all the better. Besides, it didn't pay to let men know she was just as smart as they were. Often smarter.

Ima loved site visits. They got her out of the office she so assiduously and efficiently managed, gave her a break from meetings and phone calls. But it wasn't just that. She loved the smell of wet cement and plaster and sawdust; the stacks of slates and tiles awaiting their moment, sheets of plasterboard, rolls of scrim, the stream of sparks from an angle grinder, the ringing sound of a trowel splitting a brick. The way the building came together, from a hole in the ground to a home. It never lost its allure, this sense of something in the making.

Site visits were also when she felt on an almost equal footing with Phil. It was his scheme, of course; he was the architect, but although he didn't defer to her, he consulted and listened and valued her opinion. A passion for design, detail and finishes was what drew them together. It was their area of intimacy.

She took the opportunity of the builder's chat with Phil to have a smoke. Phil loathed smoking and wouldn't kiss her if she smelled of tobacco. There were occasions, when it was a clear choice between him and tobacco, when she opted for an evening home alone so she could smoke in peace. Her relationship with Phil mirrored her relationship with cigarettes. Both were habits she repeatedly vowed to break - but not yet. Both were bad for her self-esteem. The affair was secret, at Phil's insistence. Ima had only confided in one friend and she didn't hide the fact that she thought Ima should dump Phil.

Every time you talk about Phil, Ima, in every story you tell about him, he always comes up short. Always.

Ima laughed drily.

Well, not quite. He always gives me enough rope, I'll say that for him.

She ground out the cigarette on the bare concrete floor, wondering which would be harder to renounce, Phil or tobacco.

This must be the tenant, Phil said. A pallid young woman with a nose ring and a small child in a pushchair stood in the doorway. The child was mewling. Ima studied the girl, who was barely out of her teens, but paid no attention to the child. Children didn't interest her. She wasn't about to start cooing over some teen's baby.

You must be Caitlin, Phil said.

The girl nodded. She took a packet of tobacco from her pocket and rolled a cigarette. Phil glanced at the unhappy child.

Never stops crying. Never, Caitlin said. It's doing my head in. Seriously.

Phil did his best to look sympathetic, but he didn't much care for kids either. He showed her round what would be her flat, explaining the layout, helping her visualise her future home. When they got to the bathroom he held up two tiles, one bluish-grey, the other greenish-grey.

These are for the walls, he said. Which do you prefer?

Caitlin shrugged.

I don't know. What do you think?

It's your bathroom, Ima said. It's up to you.

She tried to sound encouraging but the girl looked at her blankly as if she'd only just noticed she was there.

What if I choose one and then later I don't like it?

Phil glanced at Ima, took a deep breath.

Then I guess you'll just have to live with it.

At one of its many meetings the housing co-op members had voted to remove the barrier between architect and client and break away from paternalism. The problem was the people they housed were socially disadvantaged, not to say marginal, and weren't accustomed to being asked their opinion.

You give people a choice and they won't commit, Phil said, after the girl had gone. Most people don't know what they want, then they complain later that they don't like what they've been given. It's like what Henry Ford said: if I'd asked people what they wanted they'd have said they wanted a faster horse.

It's called democracy, Ima said.

Asking people to make decisions when you haven't given them the tools to make a meaningful decision isn't democracy, it's just more tokenism.

There were a lot of things Phil dismissed as tokenism. Positive discrimination, for example. The only thing we should positively discriminate for is merit, he said, as though a private education and being the son of a high court judge didn't give you a head start.

Diane was there when they got back to the office, just hanging around the way she did. Diane was Phil's wife. Was and is, because although they were separated, they hadn't divorced. Their relationship was neither amicable nor hostile, but they seemed to need something from each other. They spoke most days on the phone and constantly sought the other's approbation. There was an offhandedness between them that seemed forced, the way people who are having an office affair try to deflect attention by studiously showing little interest in each other while simultaneously finding excuses to be together. Except Phil and Diane weren't having an affair, they were married.

Hi Diane, Ima said. What brings you here?

Nothing special. I was in the area and thought I'd just pop in and say hi.

Liar, Ima thought. You just hang around in case anyone forgets that you're a founding member of the co-op and Phil's ex.

Coffee?

Thanks, that would be great.

It bothered Ima that, although Phil was separated from his wife, she felt more like his mistress than his sort of girlfriend. The arrangement was one-sided and old fashioned, like something from another era.

What's the story with Diane? Ima asked one morning over coffee. She held her breath. Phil didn't respond well to direct questioning.

Story?

It's just that, you're separated, so there must be a reason for that, some bad blood or something. You must have had a falling out. You never told me what happened. I know it's none of my business, well, it sort of is, isn't it? But.

But what?

You seem very close.

We are very close.

But close like inseparable.

Phil pursed his lips. Ima knew she was close to the line but she went ahead and crossed it anyway.

To be honest, the way she behaves, she's quite proprietorial. Like she doesn't want to let you go.

Are you sure it's her who's being proprietorial? he said coldly.

Diane didn't know about Ima's affair with Phil. No one did, aside from the one friend Ima had told. Phil was obsessively secretive. Ima suspected he didn't want Diane to find out because she'd be jealous and he feared her disapproval. He needn't have worried, Ima was discreet and, besides, Diane was much too wrapped up in herself to notice much about anyone else.

Ima brought the coffee to Diane who had pulled a chair up beside Phil's drawing board. She was speaking to him in an undertone, then stopped as Ima approached. The hushed tones were her way of saying, even if we're separated, he's still mine. Well, not exactly, Ima thought, and if he's so fucking precious to you why did you leave him for that guy that everyone but you could see was a total schmuck and a waster?

Thanks so much, Ima. Very kind.

No problem. It's the little things that make us great.

Diane looked puzzled. Like Phil, she was the sort of posh type who is immune to irony, asides and sardonic remarks.

Phil tells me you had dinner with Stacy McDonnell. What was she like?

Ima winced. Was she having a dig? She wondered

how much Phil had told Diane. It hadn't been a good night. Or rather, she thought it was a good night until Phil scolded her – punished her, more like – for showing him up and making a fool of herself. On the other hand, how could she show him up when their relationship was practically a state secret?

They were in the Ivy, her and Phil, writer of the moment Stacy McDonnell, along with her agent, a guy from the Architectural Association and a French woman who worked for Amnesty. It was a cool crowd, the sort Ima liked and sought to impress. She was on a roll, at her witty, pithy best, tossing out anecdotes like a series of hors d'oeuvres. She had the floor, and for a moment imagined herself like Dorothy Parker holding court in the Algonquin.

But Phil kept giving her looks and he was silent in the taxi home. He could generally be relied on to bring her down when she was on a high. When the taxi pulled up at her place he didn't get out. He said goodnight – no kiss – and gave the driver his home address.

The first thing he said the next morning at work was, you do realise how pissed you were last night, don't you?

A little frisky, she said. But nothing disgraceful, surely?

They were laughing at you.

Really? I thought they were laughing *with* me.

They were. At first.

That stung. She doubted it was true and suspected Phil was jealous that people found her more amusing than him. But it stung nonetheless. There was nothing Ima dreaded more than making a fool of herself, as Phil was well aware.

Yes, we were at the Ivy, Ima said to Diane. Stacy's very sweet, and really quite humble, given all the attention she's getting. Can't say I'm a big fan of her writing, though. I couldn't finish her last book.

Diane, whom Ima knew perfectly well was a huge Stacy McDonnell fan, gave her a distant smile as much to say, although it was me who brought the subject up, it doesn't mean I want to have a conversation with you. Ima took the hint.

At home later, Ima laid clothes out on the bed, thinking of what to pack for the weekend away with Phil which he'd finally agreed to after a lengthy campaign.

I don't get why you're so keen on this, he said.

It's what people do, Phil. Go away together. Stay somewhere nice where someone else makes the bed. We could pretend we're having a relationship.

It was left to Ima to organise, of course. She booked them into a chic hotel that had featured in both Marie Claire and Icon. She even made the two-hour drive to check it out lest she discover some naff detail that might annoy Phil and ruin the weekend. She bought a dress she couldn't afford from Paul Smith and a new one-piece in case they used the hotel pool.

Ima invested a lot in appearances. It was important that she be seen as a serious person but not someone who took herself too seriously. The trick was to downplay her sense of style, just as she concealed her intelligence under a patina of knowing self-mockery. Stylish clothes should be debunked, worn well but with a sense of irony. Which was why she wore a blatantly vulgar necklace with a chic Agnès B shirt. Or in her small apartment, which aspired to a Bauhausian Japanese minimalism, she arranged a kitsch Elvis Presley throw cushion on the Rietveld Zig Zag chair that had cost her almost a month's salary.

She and Phil shared a taste for a cool, almost austere, aesthetic, but while her apartment was all immaculate understatement, his was like a student flat. There were unwashed dishes in the sink and dirty clothes on the floor. She doubted it was like that when he still lived with Diane. Back when Ima used to stay with him, she would spend the first hour cleaning up – she couldn't help herself. After that, she stopped going and they spent their nights together at her place.

Two days before they were due to go away for their weekend together, Phil cancelled.

It's this competition, he said. The closing date is next Tuesday.

But you knew that months ago. You knew that when I booked the hotel.

I know, I thought I'd be done by now. I've been flat out.

Flat out going to a play at the National last night, flat out having dinner with Diane the night before.

You know how important this is to me, he said, not taking the bait.

Yes, and I can see how unimportant spending time with me is.

There was no point arguing. She had no real call on how much time they spent together. Phil had never said, these are my terms; he didn't need to. It was understood, he had the power, he called the shots. The way he saw it, they were both free to do as they pleased.

If he didn't want to do something he didn't do it. I don't expect you to do things you don't want to do, do I? he said. She didn't see it that way. There were things she'd like them to do together, things she hoped he'd want to do, like spending a weekend away together in a very cool hotel. Ima learnt early on that if she pushed, Phil pulled away. The only real power she had was the power of refusal, even though denying him meant denying herself.

It's too late to get a refund, she said.

Tell me how much I owe you.

More than you'll ever know, she said, stalking off before he got to see that he'd made her cry.

An hour later she got a message: Really sorry I messed up. Was hoping you might help me with the submission. You know I value your judgment.

That was as near as he got to humble pie. Flattering her so she'd do something that was in his interest, appealing to their shared love of good design. After all, there'd be no kudos for her if he won the competition. She waited exactly one hour before she replied: I'm upset and disappointed. I've made other plans for the weekend. Maybe free on Sunday afternoon if that helps.

This was a lie. She had no other plans. She spent the weekend cleaning and watching TV. Phil came over to her place on Sunday and together they went through his design for the competition. He listened to her comments and even made some modifications based on what she said. She felt included, valued, part of Phil's life, happy, almost. They ate dinner at a place nearby and she invited him to stay the night.

Ima undressed in the bathroom. She brushed her teeth, put in her diaphragm and emerged wearing a nightdress. She wasn't prudish and she was in good shape but at thirty-nine she thought dim lighting and Phil's imagination were probably an improvement on reality. When she turned off the bathroom light Phil was in bed, undressed down to his underwear which he always wore until she got in beside him. He thought the black Calvin Kleins he habitually wore were cool. She thought they were naff, but didn't say so.

He was an efficient though not affectionate lover. In bed he showed the same attention to detail he gave to floor finishes and window furniture. He never came before her, nor with her either. She was left feeling done – in the culinary sense – if not exactly loved.

Weeks passed. She didn't rebook the weekend and he didn't ask her to. On the next site visit she noticed the pipe fall had been corrected but didn't comment. The work was nearing completion. Meanwhile, Phil's design had been shortlisted for the competition. They celebrated in bed with a bottle of Krug and she let him do whatever he wanted with her.

She didn't leave Phil and she didn't stop smoking. Life went on as before until she went to the doctor for a routine check-up.

So, all OK? Ima asked as the doctor tapped notes two-fingered into a computer.

Did you know you were pregnant? she asked, glancing up from the keyboard.

Ima's lips parted, closed then parted again.

Oh, was all she said.

I see, the doctor said. So not something you planned.

Planned? Ima had spent her adult life fastidiously avoiding just this situation.

Give it time to sink in, the doctor said. Come back in a week and we'll talk about antenatal care. Assuming you wish to continue with the pregnancy.

Antenatal? More like anti-natal, Ima thought. What on earth would I do with a baby?

For practical, pragmatic Ima, there was no question. She'd have an abortion. But on the walk home she was ambushed at every turn by babies. On a park bench a young mother opened her shirt, exposing her breast. The nipple was huge and swollen. There was an elemental beauty about it, but also something grotesque, Ima felt; the veined breast full of milk, the dark, distended nipple filling the child's tiny mouth. That's what they're for, after all, Ima thought, not just for fondling or squeezing into a bikini top.

The woman in front of her in the queue for the cash machine was heavily pregnant, as was the woman in the bakery. Suddenly there were pregnant women and babies at every turn: babies in utero, in the street, in pushchairs, at the checkout, in the market, on the metro, chortling, wailing, sleeping babies – everywhere. Had they always been there? She supposed so, but she hadn't noticed them before. Now the world seemed peopled by babies, a plague of babies taunting and goading her: go on, you can have one too, you know you want to.

Except Ima had never wanted children. None of it – pregnancy, childbirth, motherhood – had ever appealed to her. All that chaos, the demands, the anxiety, never mind what childbirth does to your looks. When the subject came up, as it did from time to time, she said, it's not that I don't like children, it doesn't really interest me. There are plenty of them already. We don't all have to have them, do we?

She knew women of her age who had missed the boat, or worried they'd missed it, who'd never quite managed to get their careers, a willing partner and their fertility together on the same page. Some were disappointed, regretful; some clearly felt or were made to feel unfulfilled, but not all of them. It wasn't such a big deal these days, there were a lot of women without kids. And yet here she was, thirty-nine years old. She hadn't missed the boat. She was five weeks pregnant with a baby she didn't want. A baby she hadn't thought she might want.

When she got home, she poured a glass of wine and lit a cigarette. She sat at the kitchen table, twirled the glass by the stem. What would Phil say? He wouldn't want any part of it, she was sure of that. He'd assume she'd have an abortion. He would offer to pay, somewhere private and discreet; no one need ever know.

He was right, of course, it made no sense. But she was having trouble making sense and found it impossible to think straight above the noise her body was making. She didn't want to get pregnant, it was an accident, or carelessness perhaps. It happened and now it had to be undone. But from the moment the doctor gave her the news she'd been in the grip of something more visceral. Was that the hormones already or was it her imagination? She had the sensation of being ambushed, emotionally and physically, as though for the past thirty-nine years this was what her body had been waiting for, ready to pounce.

She looked at the glass of wine and thought, I shouldn't be drinking, for the child's sake. The thought startled her. She was pregnant, that was a condition; a child was the outcome. She stubbed out the half-smoked cigarette. The idea of the creature planted inside her, growing inside her, a thought that had always slightly disgusted her, began to tug at her heart and creep into her thoughts. You're thirty-nine, this is probably your last crack at motherhood, a voice said. Since when did I want to have a crack at it? she replied. I'd be a terrible mother. She had a vision of the apartment, toys and clutter everywhere, clothes drying, nappies, sticky fingerprints on the Rietveld chair. No, it was a crazy idea. What was she thinking? She took a large, defiant sip of wine and lit another cigarette.

On top of everything else she was angry. She wasn't careless, ever. She was diligent to the point of obsession with contraception. She was in control. She was angry with Phil, because he took no precautions and assumed it was her problem and her responsibility. She opened another bottle of wine. It was a declaration of intent. And yet the more she drank, the more her will faltered. A woman who had always plotted her course and navigated by certainties, she found herself adrift in a fog of doubt.

The choice was binary; Option A for Abortion, Option B for Baby. Option B meant total upheaval. OK, the maternity leave was generous, she helped draw up the contract herself. But even so, think of the disruption, Ima, she said to the kitchen wall, not to mention the responsibility. This isn't you; it really isn't. Your life will never be the same again. She agreed. She was swayed by the simplicity of Option A. Easy enough to arrange. A small wound to add to the inventory of other small wounds. It was the sensible option. She wouldn't tell Phil, he didn't need to know, and besides he'd be cross that she'd been so careless. It would have been her carelessness, of course. She would deal with it herself, just as she always did. So just get it done, she said, and then we can move on, back to normal. Except this took the shine off normal.

Her phone buzzed with a text message. It was Phil. Hi, everything ok? Thought I might pop round this evening if that's OK. Pop round meant he fancied a fuck. She didn't answer. She always answered, but not this time. Let him stew, even if he doesn't know why.

She woke up hungover. Her first thought was, oh my god, I'm pregnant. She made coffee and took an ibuprofen, both of which she had some vague idea were out of bounds when pregnant. She felt her breasts in the shower. Were they bigger? Had her nipples always been that dark?

You're not having a baby, she said to the bathroom mirror. That was just the wine talking, right? Right. She'd get rid of it. It made sense. Of course, it did. She'd call the doctor. The ante-natal stuff won't be necessary, thanks. I've decided not to go ahead with it.

What Ima hadn't anticipated was that the man she saw when she got to the office was not Phil her colleague and sort of boyfriend, but an altogether unfamiliar and improbable figure: Phil, the father of her unborn child. She looked at him and thought, with total clarity and equally total confusion: I'm carrying your child. Phil was flipping through a brochure of casement stays. He looked up.

Everything OK? I sent you a message last night.

Yes, sorry. I turned my phone off. Didn't see it till this morning.

Are you alright? You look anxious.

Fine. All good. Busy day. Auditors coming at eleven.

Phil nodded and went back to the brochure but Ima just stood there, the words I'm carrying your child repeating themselves like a song lyric that got stuck in her head.

The two bathroom tiles, bluish-grey and greenish-grey, lay beside Phil's drawing board. Ima ran her finger over them.

So, which did she choose in the end?

Phil looked up.

Neither. She wanted white. White in the bathroom and white in the kitchen. And white walls. White on white. Like a bloody clinic. Honestly, I wonder sometimes why we bother?

That's a little harsh. She's just a kid.

Yeah, a kid with a kid. How's that going to play out, I wonder?

Ima squeezed back the tears until she was in the bathroom. Why are you crying? she asked herself. Because he said kid? Just the word kid? Is that how it's going to be from now on? She felt like a loaded gun; anything could set her off. She sat in the cubicle and listed all the reasons she couldn't have a child. Her career, her neat, stylish home, which was too small anyway, being a single mother. Half the people they housed were single mothers; it didn't look much like fun. She brought her parents into the frame to bolster her case. Her mother would be upset, but she'd probably come around, pleased she had a grandchild at last. Not her father, though, a god-fearing drinker, always on his high horse. He'd probably never speak to her again.

What it came down to was choosing between regrets. Which decision would she regret most? To have or have not?

The thought kept coming around that what bothered her most about Phil was the way he withheld himself. She never asked much from him but whatever she asked, he held back. Now she had something of his, a piece of him; his baby. She was overwhelmed with the urge to tell him, but he'd only put pressure on her to get rid of it. Maybe she needed that pressure though. Maybe that would help her to think straight.

But did she want to think straight? Wasn't she tempted to give in to the force majeure of the thing? One reason she didn't want to tell Phil was knowing he might succeed in talking her out of it. OK, she hadn't planned it, she'd never seriously entertained the idea, but here it was. So, what then? Go ahead with it and not tell Phil. How would that work once she started to show? Oh that, oh right, I'm carrying your baby. I forgot to mention it. Sorry, it must have slipped my mind.

Ima dried her eyes. You really are a mess, she said to the mirror. She was, and yet, even though she couldn't make up her mind what to do, she felt unexpectedly empowered. There was the baby, or not. It was her choice. With Phil she had always been subject or, worse, abject. But this was her call and hers alone.

She took Phil some contracts to sign. He signed them and handed them back. She hesitated. Phil raised a quizzical eyebrow.

I'm pregnant, she said.

For a moment he looked like he'd misheard, or she'd something in a foreign language. But she fixed her grey-green eyes on him until he was in no doubt he'd heard correctly.

Should I assume …?

That it's yours? Why do men always say that? Of course, it is. It was an accident, but these things happen. I'm carrying your child. I think that's a better way of putting it, don't you, better than saying I'm pregnant? Saying I'm pregnant makes it sound like I'm unwell, as though I had the flu or bronchitis, something where you could say, don't worry, it will clear up after a while.

Ima felt almost giddy with empowerment. The firmness of purpose, the clarity, these were the qualities that had got her where she was and what people admired about her. But up till now she'd always deployed her abilities in someone else's cause. Now she was doing it for herself.

Almost overnight, Phil had lost his allure. Right then she understood that it was over between them. Maybe they could have a new and different relationship, but not this one. It wasn't that she felt nothing for him, but now her feelings had taken a new direction. He was the father of her child, the donor of twenty-three chromosomes. That made him special in a different way. An affair can end, one or both parties can break it off, but this was a living biological fact, it had substance.

Due Diligence

I used to dream that one day I'd have a house by the sea, Suzanne said. But I ended up by the river instead.

She was small woman, barely five foot high, diminished by illness, with bright eyes and a broad smile, a silver-topped cane taking her weight, not that there was much to take.

Below them the light from the windows of a line of buses on Chelsea Bridge was reflected in the dark sheen of the Thames.

What a fabulous view, Hester said.

Isn't it? It's soothing, like the sea, the rise and fall of the tides, the boats going by. There's something soulful about the Thames. I remember when it was still a working river, when I was a child. The coal barges used to come all the way up here to the power station.

Sweet Thames, run softly, till I end my song, Hester said, then immediately felt foolish, quoting poetry. Pretentious. She was conscious at this, their first meeting, of their age difference; Suzanne was twice her age. If Hester was going to persuade her to talk, she'd have to earn not just her trust, but her respect. But she wasn't going to earn it by trying to impress or being clever.

For now, they stood there silent, looking out over the river, Suzanne and Hester, two women, one expected to give, the other hoping to receive. A party boat passed under the bridge, all lit up. Inside people were dancing.

My father said he named me after that song, Suzanne. You know, Suzanne takes you down to her place by the river, she half spoke, half sang the words. He said that when he was young, the Suzanne in the song was his dream woman – artistic, mysterious, a free spirit, defiant. Which was all very well but what he needed in real life was someone to wash his socks and cook his dinner, which was where my mother came in.

Charming but disarmingly direct, that's what people said about Suzanne. Well, she was off to a good start. The little Hester knew about Suzanne was public knowledge: daughter of internationally acclaimed painter and sculptor Francis Spillane, she herself was an award-winning graphic designer. Specialises in typography; gift for logos. Divorced, no children. Cancer. Not living with but dying of, probably sooner than later. Most common epithets: charming, acid, direct, warm, mordant, generous, kind.

The little Suzanne knew about Hester was that she was born and raised in London by her mother who taught English in a secondary school in Deptford. No mention of a father. First in art history at Bristol University. Former arts correspondent on Evening Standard, now freelance. Author of book about the Arts and Crafts movement. Now working on biography of Suzanne's famous artist father. Most common epithets: quiet, bright, competent, a bit solemn; solemn being the worst anyone has to say about her.

So, Suzanne said. Where shall we begin? Maybe a drink would help?

Hester glanced at her watch, which was small and elegant and gold. Present from a boyfriend, Suzanne thought, then spotted the gold band on Hester's left hand. Correction: present from husband.

My rule has always been, no alcohol before 7pm, Suzanne said, but what the hell, I don't have time to drink myself to death, death's already got a head start.

Hester flinched.

I'm sorry. I'm dying, we both know that. I accept it and, as you seem to be along for the ride, I need you to as well.

Hester nodded.

Besides, it seems that I'm addicted to morphine now, so a drink will hardly make much difference. I know it's early but it's already dark, so we can pretend it's night time, if that makes it easier. I'll have a vodka and tonic, just the one, she said, pointing to a wall-mounted vitrina. Plenty of ice and don't stint on the vodka. Help yourself to whatever you fancy. There's white wine in the fridge.

That evening they didn't talk about Suzanne's father or the biography Hester had been commissioned to write. Much of the time they didn't say anything. They just sat by the window with their drinks watching the traffic on the bridge and Chelsea Embankment. Suzanne took some tablets from a plastic box with compartments marked with the days of the week. She washed them down with the vodka tonic. When she struggled to get to her feet Hester reached out to help her up but she waved her away.

Thank you, that's kind, but as long as I can do things for myself, I'm determined to do them. I'm not ready to throw in the towel. I'm tired now so I'm going to take myself off to bed. No, don't get up. Finish your drink. You can let yourself out. So, tomorrow, same time? We can talk then. I'm sorry, but I'm too weary tonight.

So how did it go? Hester's wife asked when she got home. Hey, have you been drinking?

Professional courtesy, Hester said. Don't worry, I'm not turning into a daytime drinker. Or not yet. It was OK, just sort of sniffing each other out, breathing each other in. We didn't talk much but she seems comfortable with silence. She's so frail, I feel bad. Like a bird of prey circling a dying animal.

Why should you feel bad? She agreed to meet you. She doesn't have to talk to you if she doesn't want to.

She has a wounded look in her eyes. You know that look in a child's eyes when it's been scolded. I had an urge to put my arm around her to comfort her, but she'd probably hate that. She's very proud and stoic. She's dying, after all. I'm going back tomorrow. Let's see if she'll open up. I know I have to be patient, but I'm so conscious that I don't have much time. Or rather, she doesn't.

The following day Suzanne was a little brighter.

It's hard to strike an equilibrium between being in pain and feeling numb. Numb as in numbskull, she laughed.

I have a question.

I'm sure you do. Isn't that why you're here?

You told me your father named you after that Leonard Cohen song. But you were born ten years before he wrote it.

Suzanne laughed.

That's very observant of you, and of course you're absolutely right. But my father only ever had a passing relationship with the truth. He'd say things because he liked the sound of them. Hardly anyone challenged him so he got away with all sorts of nonsense.

Artistic licence.

You could say that. The less generous tend to call it bullshit. Tell me about yourself, Hester.

There's not much to tell.

Why do people always say that? Of course, there is.

Hester trotted out a brief biography. Suzanne listened attentively. She was a good listener.

You're obviously close to you mother, Suzanne said when she'd finished. But you haven't mentioned your father.

I never knew my father.

Interesting. Here we are, two women, one with a dominating, egotistical father, the other with no father at all. I wonder which of us has come off worse. You're married, aren't you?

Hester nodded.

Tell me about your husband.

Wife, Hester corrected her, which earned her an amused half smile. I assume that's not a problem.

Not at all. We'd all be lesbians if we had any sense. How did you meet?

It was quite corny really. I was her waitress. I worked in a restaurant for a while.

And so this woman who is now your wife?

Natalia.

Natalia picked you up in a restaurant.

Sort of. We just chatted, but it was obvious she was flirting. She left her business card with the bill, with the words Call me.

Nice touch.

That's what I thought. I waited a day, then I called her.

And I bet you've kept that card, haven't you?

Hester nodded and blushed.

You're a romantic. That's good. I'm beginning to like you, Hester. I think we'll get along fine.

Good, but the thing is, we're supposed to be talking about you, not me.

Plenty of time for that, she said, although time was one thing Suzanne didn't have plenty of.

Hester's visits never lasted more than a couple of hours before Suzanne was overcome by exhaustion or pain or morphine. Sometimes she dozed off in mid-sentence. Each night when Hester got home and listened to the recording or read her notes, what she had was some more or less amusing stories, some quite rambling thanks to the morphine, but nothing much she could actually use, that is, little about Suzanne's father, which was why she was there. She often went off at a tangent, like the time she asked Hester if she suffered from penis envy.

Of course not, Suzanne answered for her. And yet thanks to Freud, much of the dominant thinking in psychiatry has centred on the idea that what women want, what really bothers us, is not having a cock. I mean, really, Hester, have you ever for one single moment wished you had a cock?

No, never, Hester chuckled. But I've often wished for some of the advantages that having one brings.

There you go. If we want to be like men, it's only because we want to be treated as their equal, not because we want what is frankly the ugliest and perhaps the silliest part of the human anatomy.

They giggled. It was fun, but it wasn't what Hester was after. Then one evening – this was maybe her fifth or sixth visit - Suzanne started talking about her brother. It felt like some sort of a breakthrough.

After my brother graduated, he left, Suzanne said. Just like that, like it was the obvious next stage – school, university, gone. There's no room for me here, he said. There's no room for anyone. Dad uses up all the available light. Nothing can grow in his shadow.

The streets below them were sleek with rain and the black cabs shimmered like beetles as they crawled over the bridge. The river was hypnotic. It drew you in, stealing your thoughts. Like an open fire, you could watch it for hours and let time roll by.

My brother was gone for three years, restless, travelling. He sent postcards that mostly just said, Hi from Singapore or Lima or wherever. He came back but he never really returned. He was here but he wasn't, if you see what I mean. He'd call round to see my mother, usually when he knew my father wasn't around. She was glad to see him but hurt by his distance. She used to say,

I don't know what I did to drive that boy away. She knew it wasn't her who drove him away, but loyalty to my father stopped her saying it, or maybe even thinking it.

Your brother and father didn't get along then?

It wasn't so much that they didn't get along. They went through the motions, at least. But my brother was quicker than me to see that my father's encouragement and approval was never going to be forthcoming so he never sought it. He was right, of course. Successful people are driven and single-minded. They're not always a lot of fun to be around. People say: he sacrificed everything for his art. You could delete the word everything and replace it with everyone.

Is that how you feel, that you've been sacrificed, or you sacrificed yourself for your father's art?

Suzanne shrugged.

The question is, as I see it, is it possible to be both great and good? she said. It seems to me that if you really pursue greatness, if you really keep your eyes on the prize, and it doesn't matter much what the prize is, whether it's winning Wimbledon or a Nobel or a Pulitzer, there isn't much room for anyone else or their feelings. Empathy doesn't get a look in. And when you live with someone who's driven like that, you can't escape from their shadow. I am and will always be known firstly as Francis Spillane's daughter and only secondly as myself, despite having a successful career in my own right. I've learnt to live with that. My brother took off and I often thought about doing the same, to get out from under that shadow, but in the end, I decided to try to cut myself a clearing rather than escape from the dark woods. I also stayed out of loyalty to my mother. Someone had to.

OK, Hester thought, now we're getting somewhere.

And you did make a clearing. You're a lot more than Francis Spillane's daughter.

Ha! It's true and it's nice of you to say it, but let's face it, the reason you're here talking to me is because I'm his daughter, not because of anything I achieved.

OK, fair comment. But that doesn't diminish your own work. You must be proud of what you've achieved?

Yes, I am proud of my work. Some of it, at least. But what it took me a long time to realise, and clearly my brother already had this figured out, was that my father didn't want us to get out from under his shadow. He didn't want us to shine. I was well into my thirties before I understood that my father saw me and my brother as competitors, which I guess is why he never offered us any affirmation. He was afraid, or jealous, of our success and, god forbid, that we might be more successful than him. He always dismissed my work as a graphic artist because it was mostly created for commercial motives, which in his view cancelled out any artistic merit it might have. It rendered the work impure. Never mind that he made way more money than any graphic artist I know ever did. Nor that, towards the end of his life, he was painting more or less to order, for money. The way I see it, graphic art is art, if what we mean by art is expression. Typography is expressive, logos, brands - Coca-Cola, Chanel, the Nike swoosh, Apple, Rolex. They tell us something. Why else would companies guard them so fiercely? I said to him once, Andy Warhol painted the

Campbell's soup can because it was an iconic piece of graphic art. Yes, he said, it was iconic, but it was still just a soup can. But when Warhol painted it, he transformed it into art.

Your father wasn't proud of your success, then? The awards you won, the famous logos?

Suzanne laughed, then winced from the pain the laughter brought.

Long ago my brother said, forget it, Suzanne, you can't win and you never will. If you became the ruler of the universe, Dad would say, yeah, well, that's quite something, but of course the universe was bigger in my day.

Suzanne turned to face the river. Hester felt she had opened a wound. She lay a hand on her bony shoulder and then, when Suzanne didn't resist, slid her arm around her and put her head against hers, expecting to be rebuffed, which she wasn't. They sat like that, watching the river roll by.

Do you feel grown up, Hester? Suzanne asked after a while.

I don't know. Grown up, how?

When you were a little girl, you looked at people, women, and you thought, that's what I'll be one day?

Of course.

You think you'll arrive at this idea of being grown up, but it's a myth, a mirage. You become an adult, you go to work, you have a mortgage, lovers, heartbreak, success, disappointment. But part of you never grows up, part of you is forever a little girl, in my case, a little girl desperate for her father's approval. Just a word, one sodding little word of praise. Whatever I've done, my triumphs great and small, I'm inhabited, possessed, by that silently imploring little girl. It's arrested development, that's what it is, the inner child holds us back, drags us back to something we can never escape. People talk a lot about their inner child, as though it were some personal garden of Eden. But you know what? If I could get my hands on my inner child, I'd wring her neck.

Hester didn't know what to say to that, but she didn't have to say anything. Suzanne's chin dropped and she dozed against Hester's shoulder. Hester watched the play of flashing blue lights on the river as a police car weaved through the traffic on the embankment.

The next couple of visits weren't fruitful from Hester's point of view. Suzanne was obviously in a lot of pain and was drowsy from the drugs. They spoke little and spent most of the visit holding hands by the window. Then one day Suzanne was in the kitchen making scrambled eggs, one of the few things she could bring herself to eat.

You seem a lot better today, Hester said.

Good days, bad days. What about you? You seem out of sorts?

Me? No, why?

Suzanne gave her a look.

It's nothing, really.

Have you and Natalia had a fight? she said, scraping the eggs on to a plate.

You don't miss much, do you?

I miss plenty. What was the fight about?

Stupid stuff. We were talking about your father and

she went off on a number about Eric Gill.

Oh, that old chestnut. Do we judge the art by the artist or the artist by the art? The problem is we want the people we admire to deserve our admiration, then we feel cheated when we discover our favourite actors or singers or sports stars are stupid or racist or simply rather dull. I assume Natalia was saying that, because Eric Gill raped his daughters, it devalues his art.

Well, it kind of does, doesn't it? Especially if you look at it from the daughters' point of view.

Absolutely, which is why it's best not to know too much about your heroes. They'll only let you down. We know that Tolstoy regularly screwed the young peasant women on his estate, impregnating an unknown number of them. We know that Victor Hugo had a penchant for prostitutes and Rousseau put all five of his children into an orphanage while writing about how to improve education. We say, what hypocrites you are, practise what you preach, put your money where your mouth is. But *Anna Karenina* is still a masterpiece. And Rousseau really did change the way we think about education.

So you think you can separate the two, the art and the artist?

It's a conundrum. *Anna Karenina* is a great book written by a man who regularly forced himself on defenceless women who depended on him for their livelihood. A rapist, in short. Flawed genius or a bad man – or just a man? If you can't enjoy *Anna Karenina* because of the sort of man Tolstoy was, fair enough. Totally understandable. But nothing changes the fact that *Anna Karenina* is a masterpiece.

What Natalia was saying was that just because someone makes great art it doesn't mean we have to forgive them for how they treat the people around them?

And she's right. Imagine yourself, a woman, telling some wretched serf on Tolstoy's estate with one of his little bastards sucking on her scrawny breast, oh, don't feel bad, you got knocked up by a great writer. All I'm saying is it's up to you to separate the art from the artist, or not. I never said anything about forgiveness. Forgiveness is a private affair. Besides, we live in stern times, these days no one is forgiven for their sins, however long ago they were committed. One shameful act, one unfortunate remark, even said or done when drunk or very young, and that's you finished. One strike and you're out, a lifetime's work tarnished and devalued. Notoriety doesn't sell any more. And while we're on the subject of notoriety, I've been thinking, and I'm saying this now because I don't want to waste your time, there's something I should tell you.

Hester tilted her head in receiver mode.

Just so you know, my father never sexually abused me. You can cross that off your list. I mean, if you're after an Eric Gill story, sorry, can't help you there.

Is that what you think, Suzanne, that I'm here to get some dirt on your father?

I don't think ill of you, Hester, but isn't that what your publisher wants? You're an art historian, I'm sure you'll write something scholarly about my father's work, not that you'll be the first. But you're not here to talk about the work, are you? It's the man you want to talk about, you want me to tell you what sort of man he was.

Fair enough. I'm after what the newspaper business calls colour. A portrait of the artist.

But some dirt would help sales. It always does. The sort of colour that paints him as a loving husband and father and all-round sweet man who wouldn't hurt a fly doesn't sell so well. And I'm sure you already know enough about my father to know that as a family we've not exactly been like the Waltons, and therefore there must be, if not actual dirt, some unpleasantness to report.

Hester discovered early on that no one in the art world was willing to dish the dirt on Spillane, or not in public and on the record. Spillane was their currency and they didn't want to see it devalued by some unfortunate revelation about his personal beliefs or predilections. Suzanne was right, these were unforgiving times.

I'm not here to pry, Hester said.

What else does a biographer do, if not pry? Suzanne said. But she was smiling.

That evening at home Hester burst into tears over dinner.

What is it, hon?

I don't know, I can't explain, she said when she'd dried her eyes. It's just so raw, her pain, everything about her. It's like she's emotionally naked but she covers up. No self-pity, no resentment. She's so loyal, loyalty is a shibboleth to her. She doesn't say it, but it's what comes across. It's this sense I have of being with someone who is good, a really good person, what you'd call a good soul, who's been hurt, dismissed, wronged. And in spite of that, somehow her goodness is there, intact, resolute, constant. She talks around her father but without ever saying anything directly about him. But he's there, a presence, he overshadows everything. Like doom personified.

That's probably a reflection of how she dealt with him when he was alive, don't you think? The way women tiptoe around men so they don't get angry or beat them up. Or do you think she's holding back? Maybe there is some scandal.

My feeling is that there isn't, but I could be wrong. She's very open with me, but at the same time she doesn't give much away. Yesterday she said, there's only one thing you need to know about my father, and I thought, oh great, here we go. But you know what she said? He was a man. That's all you need to know, Hester, he was a man.

Is that like her saying, you know what they're like, they're all the same?

Maybe, or it could be the morphine. She gets a bit fuzzy round the edges.

Suzanne gave her keys.

There are days when it's such an effort to get up, so you can let yourself in. Besides, I might be dead. You could be the first with the news. Bit of a scoop.

I wish you wouldn't talk like that.

I'm sorry, am I too flippant?

It's not that. But I've become quite fond of you, so I'd rather you held off dying for as long as possible.

There was a notebook on the table, the page held open with a pen. The notebook was cloth-bound, with marbled endpapers and unlined pages, the sort you used to find in specialist stationers in Holborn or the City.

What are you writing? Hester asked.

My diary. Do you keep a diary?

I used to. When I was a girl, and a teenager, like a lot of girls. But I gave it up when I went to university.

I never did. It just became a habit. I suppose I thought if I didn't write things down they'd be forgotten. And yet I've never once gone back and reread them. I don't even read what I wrote yesterday.

Have you kept them all?

Of course. Well, I say of course, but I could just as well throw them out. As I said, I never read them.

Someone else might, though.

Really, why?

For Hester, the discovery that Suzanne had kept a diary throughout her life was like finally finding the word that's been on the tip of your tongue

Well, I'm thinking that maybe your father's story isn't the one I want to tell. The more time I spend with you, the more interested I am in you and less in him. After all, your father's story has already been told one way or another; yours has not.

Suzanne laughed and waved her hand dismissively. But there was no question that she was pleased, flattered even.

This is all because I won't dish the dirt on my father, isn't it?

Not at all. I meant what I said, every word of it.

That's very sweet of you. Now please get me a drink.

Look, Suzanne said, twirling the ice in her glass with

her finger. Let's say I could tell you things that would cast my father in a bad light. Let's just suppose there are things I could say that would profoundly damage his standing as an artist. There might be some satisfaction in that, revenge for the harm he's done to me and others. But then if I did that, what would be the point of having kept silent all these years, of putting up with feeling neglected, of having your self-esteem shot down any time it found its wings? It would have all been for nothing. Above all, it would be a betrayal of my mother; he was her husband and she stuck it out, that's what women did, and still do. I'm not here to defend my father's reputation; it's my mother I'm defending. There are things I could say, but what's to be gained? Revenge, settling a few scores?

They say that happiness is the best revenge.

Do they? I like that, it has nice ring about it. Once I was old enough to think for myself, the one thing I was clear about was I didn't want to be like my father. It's not much of a goal, but I was determined not to be the sort of person who doesn't let anything get in the way of what they want, anything that might thwart their ambition. It takes an extraordinary amount of chutzpah to believe that you can behave like a complete shit and people will still love you. Not many women have that sort of confidence. We're just not made that way. You could argue that I decided there and then to forfeit any possibility of greatness in exchange for trying to be a decent human being, someone people liked rather than simply admired. You could also argue that I failed on both fronts, but there we are. My father was on his journey, my brother on his. I wasn't prepared to abandon my mother, and who else was going to stick around?

And yet this is the first time you've talked about your mother.

Is it? That's because it pains me to talk about her. Let me tell you something. My mother's death certificate states that she died of complications due to pneumonia. This isn't true. She died of disappointment. That certificate should say: died on hunger strike, because that what she did, she starved herself to death. She erased herself. Like me, she was a tiny woman, barely five foot one, so you'd think it wouldn't take much, but it did; it took years, decades. People talk about strength of will but the body is also strong, astonishingly resilient. It will survive on little, even a diet of coffee and cigarettes, for years. It resists erasure; the body has a will of its own. The force that through the green fuse drives the flower, as Dylan Thomas put it. It's powerful, seemingly unstoppable. My mother may have wished she was dead but her body was having none of it. Her hunger strike began when I was eight years old and ended when I was forty, which was when she finally died.

In ancient Ireland, people would starve themselves on the doorstep of someone who had wronged them as a way of shaming them. My mother was Irish, or at least her father was. She had that in her, that capacity for self-immolating endurance, that ferocious darkness that so many Celts carry inside them, violent and self-destructive. And by the way, if the idea was to shame my father, the person who had wronged her, I don't think it worked. The fact is she was loyal to the last. It was herself, not him, whom she punished for his betrayal.

How had he wronged her, you ask? In the most banal way, with another woman, a much younger woman. If starving yourself to death over a little infidelity seems like an over-reaction, you have to understand that mother was virtually an orphan. Her own mother died giving birth to her and her father shunted her around the aunties. Then when she was twenty, she met my father, Mr Wonderful. She devoted herself to him, his career, his art. She'd had this lonely, loveless childhood and she pinned all her colours to the mast of Mr Wonderful. When the ship went down, when he betrayed her, it was more than she could bear. She went down with the ship, but as I said, it took a long time.

She hid what she was doing. She didn't make a show of not eating. She always had an excuse at the ready: she'd just had a snack; she ate while she was cooking; her stomach wasn't quite right. Like junkies and alcoholics, she was adept at cover-ups and alibis and hiding the truth from those around her and from her doctor. Love was her best disguise. By giving so much to others, to me and my brother in particular, she distracted us from what she was doing to herself. She never let on how profoundly unhappy she was, or else as kids we just couldn't see it. We were just too wrapped up in ourselves to notice until later.

Suzanne was exhausted by this outpouring and sat, eyes half closed, slumped in her chair. Hester took the glass from her hand. She put an arm around her shoulder and sang softly: Old man river, that old man river, he don't say nothing but he must know something. Old man river, he just keeps rolling along.

The thing is, Suzanne said, suddenly awake, my father was a great artist but my mother was a great person. My father was a talker, my mother a listener. Above all, my mother loved. She gave. When I was a teenager, my friends used to come to the house to talk to my mother, even If I wasn't home. She always had time for people. She listened, sometimes she gave advice, but she never judged. Here's the thing. The day after my mother's funeral I was sitting by the window in her house. One of those grim, grey days when it doesn't even deign to rain, a lightless day when nightfall comes as a relief because at least then it's dark and you don't expect anything more of the dark than darkness. I was in one of those empty places where loss takes you, the desert between the hills and valleys of grief when you're not quite ready to start crying again and you're not really thinking anything, your brain just idling in neutral because it's impossible to switch it off and all you're doing is being because being's what's left to do. I remember a woman in a black coat passed by, dragging an uncooperative child by the hand. A man with a tattoo on his neck sat at the wheel of a van parked opposite smoking with the window down. A boy about twelve went past wearing a red football shirt, Arsenal, I only know that because it had the cannon motif. All these images have lodged in my mind. Then a chaffinch appeared on the window sill. It looked at me, first with one eye, then the other. It lowered its head, bent its neck and looked out towards the street, then back at me. It seemed to hold my gaze, and then it was gone. I'm not religious, not even slightly, and I have no firm ideas about the soul or the afterlife. But I knew that bird was my mother, come for one last goodbye. I was sure of that. Absolutely certain. It was her.

When Hester arrived the following day, some sixth sense, an ancestral, animal instinct told her that Suzanne had left the building. Even while she waited downstairs for the lift, she sensed her absence. She turned the key in the apartment door as quietly as possible, so as not to – so as not to what? She shut the door behind her with just the faintest of clicks. There was a scent of jasmine incense from a joss stick burning in a champagne glass. It had almost burnt down. Hester had never known Suzanne to burn incense.

She eased open the bedroom door and there was Suzanne, at peace in a green silk dress. She'd done her make-up. On the bedside table there was an empty blister pack of morphine tablets beside an empty water glass. Hester had never seen a dead person before but in that instant grasped the mystery, understood why every culture has an idea of the spirit or the soul. Suzanne was there and she wasn't. It made no sense. Instinctively, Hester turned to open the window, but Suzanne had already thought of that.

She sat by the window overlooking the river. Sweet Thames, run softly, till I end my song, she said aloud, and then started to cry in an effortless way; just tears, not sobs. You have to do something, she said, aloud once again. You can't just sit here with a dead woman. She couldn't think of who else to call so she called an ambulance. Not that one was needed.

There was a large cardboard box on the floor by the coffee table and she sat there for several minutes before noticing the envelope with her name on it on top of the box. Inside was a note that read: These are for you. Do whatever you choose with them, which includes doing nothing or simply throwing them in the bin. Thank you so much for seeing me out. Talking to you helped, it really did, more than you can imagine. Take care, much love, Suzanne.

Hester glanced towards the bedroom, as though seeking permission. She opened the box. Inside were Suzanne's diaries. The oldest dated from when Suzanne was just thirteen. She had kept a diary ever since. The most recent entry was from the day before. It read: Thanks, Hester. It's been a pleasure. See you around.

Hester started to cry. She went into the bedroom and sat beside what had been Suzanne. She resisted covering her face with the sheet, she didn't want to shut her way. But she closed her eyes; they weren't looking at anything, after all.

You're right, Suzanne, she said, taking her cold hand in hers. It's not about payback. Payback is an illusion. Some, probably most things can't be avenged. But there is the matter of balancing the books. What do they call it? An audit, but more than that; it's not just about profit and loss. It's about how things were done, what was done well, what badly. Not a settling of scores but seeing things in the round; credit where credit is due. Due diligence. I think that's what they call it.

Wasted and Wounded

Vincent stood at the edge of the dark meadow, peeing into the whin bushes under a starless sky. The night chill took the edge off the Bushmills. The revolving beam of the Rathlin Island lighthouse lit briefly the yellow flowers as the briney whiff of sea blended with the whins' sharp aroma and the acid odour of urine.

He was thinking about happiness. Perhaps it was out there in the depths of the implacable Antrim night. Life, liberty and the pursuit of happiness, that was the idea, and yet Vincent hadn't enough fingers to count the people he knew who were forever outrunning happiness, lured away by bad choices, bad medicine and bad love. They weren't pursuing happiness; it pursued them, red-faced and breathless, like someone running alongside a train that is forever pulling out of the station. He'd become just such a person. How had that happened? Did he really choose to be unhappy?

Vincent had chased happiness down a dead-end street for the past eight years convincing himself, in spite of all the evidence, that things would get better, that the dead end would open on to a golden highway of joy. Heartbreak would metamorphose into happiness, putting an end to eight years of lulling himself to sleep to the tune of *If Loving You Is Wrong, I Don't Want To Be Right*. But there was no way around it, he had to face the facts: it was bad love, the kind of love that makes you wretched, but a poison you keep taking because it hasn't killed you yet. It was like addiction, where the drug, any drug, retains its association with good times and feeling good long after it has ceased to do anything but drag you down into a morass of self-loathing. Before he had hope, options; now what he had was a disease. He was a fool for love. He was every poem and pop song about broken hearts and why doncha love me the way I do. But he was singing new songs now, songs about getting up and getting out and babe, I'm gonna leave you. He'd sung them before, but only under his breath. Now he was singing out loud, this time he meant it. He was going to walk away. Just watch me, he said.

Face it, Vincent, Ellie's a bitch, his friend Karen said. That was years ago, before she lost patience with him and refused to discuss it anymore.

That's unfair, she's insecure.

An insecure bitch, then, she said. But still a bitch.

Karen was a good friend, she was loyal, and she liked to tell it like it is. Maybe she was right, Ellie wasn't a nice person, or, at least, not nice to Vincent. Certainly, the evidence had been piling up for some time. But Vincent was in love. That was the problem. He was aware that there is nothing even slightly novel about being in love with someone who makes you unhappy. There are plenty of songs about that, too.

Vincent turned his back on the sea. Between him and the town there were two points of light. They came here every Easter, the whole family – mum, dad, the four kids, boyfriends and girlfriends, hangers on – a dozen or more people stuffed into a caravan designed for eight.

One point of light was the yellow rectangle of the caravan window and inside the moving shadow that was Maggie, navigating a heavy swell of Smirnoff Blue, gesticulating to make a point. The other was the dim glow of the Ford Escort's interior light where Mikey sat with his father-in-law-to-be and a bottle of Black Bush. A wisp of blue-white Embassy Regal smoke curled out through the quarter light, carried on the voice of Tom Waits singing:

Wasted and wounded,
It ain't what the moon did.
Got what I paid for now.

Inside the caravan Roberta, matriarch par excellence, perched on a stool knitting while the others were all crammed around the foldaway Formica table: the three sisters Ellie, Maggie and Susan, in that order, and kid brother Brian, plus their partners. Maggie and Susan were on the Smirnoff Blue and lemonade. Maggie's boyfriend Andy was slumped in a corner asleep. Big sister Ellie was sipping Jameson's and playing patience. Brian was on the Smithwick's while his girlfriend Rona was reading a magazine and making her vodka tonic last the evening, the way she did.

Maggie filled her glass almost to the top with vodka.

Pass the thinners, she slurred.

Susan slid the bottle of lemonade across the table.

Maggie was getting drunk. The declension of her vodka drinking went: witty and barbed – sentimental – repetitious – nasty and barbed - gone. Maggie was clever, funny and sweet until she got hammered. You could see it coming, usually around the fourth round: her head tilted to one side, her mouth turned up at one corner, her voice thickened and dropped a couple of tones, and then it was all downhill.

Whenever they were out and Maggie got loaded – which was pretty much always – Ellie looked at her sister with disdain, if she looked at her at all. Not that Ellie didn't drink, she drank plenty, but she never lost control. It was left to Vincent, once Maggie had got her fill, to take her by the arm and drag her home and fold her muttering and fully clothed into bed. For all that, he loved her in a gentle, brotherly way. It was very different from the adoring but abject love he bore for her big sister.

Mikey must be giving daddy a right ear-bashing out there, Maggie said, poking a Nº6 into the corner of her mouth and lighting up.

Sure, they've a lot to talk about, Susan said primly.

He must have locked the doors or daddy would have fled by now, so he would, Maggie said with a nasty smile.

Ach, Maggie, her mother admonished, without looking up from her knitting.

Mikey was Susan's boyfriend and he was in the Ford Escort with Gerard, his prospective father-in-law, asking for Susan's hand in marriage. Mikey and Susan had been living together for years so it was all a formality but

Mikey liked attention and it was his idea of irony to play the old-fashioned suitor and sit in the dark with Gerard drinking whiskey from plastic cups with Tom Waits on the stereo. Mikey was mad for Tom, whom he quoted often. They'd been in the car for over an hour.

Mikey could talk for Ireland. He was notorious for his rambling stories. In the pub the rest of them vied not to sit by him lest they got snared in one of his unfathomable tales. It was always the same, no matter how hard you tried to concentrate, you always lost the thread. His stories didn't seem to begin anywhere, or they started in the middle and then took off down a side road and you were never quite sure if they'd ended or why he was telling the story or if it had any point. His stories were like very long jokes with no punch line.

Brian, be a love and poke your head out the door and see if daddy doesn't need rescuing, Maggie said to her brother. Mikey will be doing daddy's head in with his stories.

You'll do no such thing, her mother said. Just let them be.

They've another four or five Tom Waits albums to get through yet, Brian said. And that's not counting the double live one.

Brian had a quiet way about him, with a nice line in gentle irony. As the only boy and the baby to boot, he'd ploughed his own corner of the family field.

Every year when they got together, the family always went for a session in the same bars, while mum and dad stayed behind. Easter in Ballycastle was the Harbour Bar; New Year's Eve in Ballyshannon was The Barracks.

Mikey and Susan were notoriously tight with money and would find ways of never paying for their round. Susan would discover she hadn't brought her purse, or Mikey would say they had to leave just before it was their turn. When it was their round they'd say, it's our round, when everyone else took their turns as individuals, not as couples. One night in the Harbour Bar, Maggie, who was already well away, bought in a round and plonked a single pint of Smithwicks in front of Mikey and Susan. There you go, she said, that's our pint.

Back in the caravan, one slender finger of vodka separated Maggie from barbed and witty and barbed and nasty. She was needling Susan, who was an easy target. Susan was thin-skinned and immune to irony. Susan and Mikey were getting married and they'd get to share a bed in the family home or a patch of floor in the caravan. This annoyed the older sisters, not because they cared about her getting married but because to them Susan was always the good girl who hadn't moved further away from the nest than Belfast, where she trained as a nurse and bought a house with Mikey. Ellie and Maggie lived in squats in London and went on marches in support of Irish political prisoners and a woman's right to choose. Susan didn't give a toss about politics.

You'd not be thinking of a white wedding, I suppose, Maggie said. A bit late for that, so it is.

Would you stop that now, Maggie, her mother said. Of course, they'll be married in St Matthew's.

Which they would, because Roberta said so and if Roberta said you got married in church, you did. Roberta wielded soft power as effectively as if she were toting an AK47. She was patient. She quietly wore people down like water smoothing a stone. You hardly felt a thing; you barely knew anything was happening at all, but she always prevailed. She had a way of making everyone feel special and singled out, which in turn made each one in turn both complicit and compliant. If she asked you to do something – ach, you wouldn't do a wee message now – you dropped what you were doing and did it. She was a classic matriarch, stern but boundlessly loving. Only a fool would risk forfeiting that love.

Roberta was the family historian and archivist. The first day back in Ireland, she gave everyone an update on who had been diagnosed with what, who was having chemotherapy, been in a car accident or, if they'd died, who was at their funeral and who was noticeably absent. She knew who was related to whom, all the degrees of separation, who was a full cousin, who once or twice removed. She seemed to have cousins in every corner of Donegal, Derry and Armagh. At new year, en route to a distant cousin's house in Rossnowlagh, they always stopped off at one of Roberta's half cousins in Belleek, a woman who talked like Molly Bloom's soliloquy at the end of Ulysses. It was a wonder listening to her. If you put what she said straight on the page you'd win the Pulitzer. She also made silky smooth but powerful poitín that she kept in Lucozade bottles. She called it the child. You'll be wanting a wee nip of the child, she'd say before they left. Keep out the cold.

In the caravan it was a case of Roberta's house, Roberta's rules. Although all four of her children lived with their partners, they weren't allowed to sleep together in the caravan or under her roof. If you weren't married, you didn't sleep together in her house, and every Easter when they all came home, Roberta rose to the challenge of devising a sexually segregated sleeping plan for a dozen people in a four-bed caravan. It was impressive. Roberta was easy to love, impossible to defy.

The flipside of acceding to Roberta's rules was they all got to behave like children. She shopped, cooked, cleaned, ironed and folded. In the morning she would produce, from the caravan's tiny stove, bacon, eggs, sausages, soda farls, barmbrack, tea and coffee for all of them. No one had to lift a finger. The older sisters, Ellie and Maggie, home from England for the holidays, regressed. Ellie played daddy's good little girl who got top marks at school while Maggie slipped into the black sheep bad girl persona she'd been trying on since she was fourteen.

Ellie always cut Vincent dead the moment they entered her parents' house and that's the way it stayed for the duration, every Christmas and Easter. She behaved as though he didn't exist. Vincent could see the logic in this: if Ellie was going to regress to being a little girl, then obviously there was no place for a boyfriend, so she treated him like a stranger. It made sense, but it hurt, and she knew it did. Maggie said not to take it personally; Ellie treated all her boyfriends the same. But how else could he take it?

It was possible that Ellie was unkind because she was insecure, obliging him to give more in return for less as proof of his devotion. Maybe, though, she was simply unkind. Right from the start there were warning signs. A close friend told him: she's charming but she's not nice. From the very beginning she tended to ignore him if they were in company, which they usually were; Ellie liked to have a lot of people around her. Vincent saw the signs but wilfully misread them, believing he was heading for somewhere that wasn't actually on the map. The problem with bad love is that by the time you see it for what it is, you're already in deep, so deep that getting out looks as daunting as staying in. Like quicksand, struggling against it only sucks you further in.

Ellie was vivacious and charismatic; everyone loved her, everyone wanted to be her friend. Like her mother, she had the knack of making people feel special and singled out for her attention while keeping them just that little bit at arm's length, leaving them wanting more. Perhaps that was why she had such a gift for getting people to do things for her, from making the tea to helping her move house. She scarcely had to ask.

When it came to getting what she wanted, men were a pushover. One time her car got towed away for being illegally parked. When they went down to the pound to retrieve it the guy in the booth told her, the same as he told everyone, no money, no car. Ellie pleaded, but no dice. So she put on a spectacular damsel in distress show, tears and everything. Vincent was embarrassed. He whispered to her to stop, she had nothing to gain from demeaning herself like this, these people had a job to do, they had rules, a system. If your car gets towed away you have to pay to get it back, end of story. And yet after a few minutes of this pathos the guy melted. He turned around and scanned the rows of car keys, handed

Ellie's hers and said: Don't worry about it, love. It was unheard of. Vincent was outraged, though relieved, as he would have ended up paying the fine.

Given that she had this power over men, she was bound to use it, and why not? She had men eating out of her hand. In Vincent's case, the trouble was she was eating the hand as well.

Ellie wanted proof of love; love was there to be tested and thus, inevitably, would be found wanting. He played along, like a mediaeval knight jousting for the lady's hand, but by passing each new test, all he proved was that the challenge must have been too easy, and so she dreamt up some new and more demanding ways for him to demonstrate his love. Vincent became aware that, as the tests became more difficult, the rewards shrank accordingly. The harder he worked, the less he got in return. Ellie presented this as sexual politics, that a man should have to earn a woman's love, not expect it. He could buy into that but what he never figured out was whether she was trying to prove that she was unlovable or that no man was worthy of her love. Either way, he'd had enough.

Vincent said to Ellie one day: You keep raising the bar.

I'm aware of that.

One day it will be too high for me to jump over it.

I know.

So, I can't win.

You're not supposed to.

That was the sort of smart, tough thing she liked to say and he liked to hear. It took the ball out of the personal and into the safer, political court. Men had always won and now that had to stop, that's what she was saying. But it was disingenuous, because it was personal. She needed him, or if not him, someone else, and needed him to need her. The returns were diminishing; the more she asked the less she was willing to give in return, including sex, which was one of his rewards for good behaviour. The more needy he became, doing more in return for less, the more abject he was in her eyes, more worthy of contempt. It was doomed. It was his fault; if she treated him with contempt it was because he let her, and if he let her, he deserved it. The end of this thought process was the realisation that he needed to get out. But every time he resolved to leave, something happened that made him hesitate.

One time, just when he'd decided to end it, Ellie suggested they go camping in France, just the two of them for a change. Vincent bought an old van and took it to a mechanic he knew.

What do you think, he asked?

Well, it goes and it's street legal.

We're planning to drive to the south of France. Do you think that's wise?

The mechanic, an Irishman whose name, Austin Heaney, destined him to live with a socket wrench in his hand, gave him a long look.

I don't know about the van but I do know I'd go anywhere with that woman and I wouldn't stop to think about it being wise, I'd just go, he said.

It was the way he said it, no nudge, no wink; he wasn't talking about sex. He was saying, do you realise how lucky you are? That threw Vincent and the little resolve he'd built up to leave her dribbled away. It kept happening. Just when he summoned up the will to leave, someone would say, Leave her? You must be crazy. He imagined confiding to the mechanic that yes, she's special, she's really got something, but you know what? she treats me like dirt. The guy either wouldn't believe him or else he'd think that, if that's how she treats you, it must be your fault. Which it mostly was.

Right down the line he told himself it would get better, that there was a brighter day around the corner. But there was no corner, he saw that now; just one long, hard and hurtful highway. He was living on the crumbs of her love. When he said, I love you, she didn't say, I love you, too, which everyone knows is the requisite reply. Then last summer they were on holiday in France, in Noirmoutier, just the two of them, which was unusual, because whenever they went on holiday, Ellie invited other people to come along, sometime a whole gang of them.

After lunch they went back to the pension and had sex - languid, post-lunch, whoozy with wine, sex. I think that may be the best sex I've ever had, he said afterwards, regretting it almost immediately. She lay on her back, looking up at the ceiling, smoking. After a while she said, I guess the best sex I ever had was with Donal. Donal was a fling she'd had one long weekend long ago in Donegal.

That should have been it. He should have upped and left. She had no money – she never did - and he should have left her there barefoot and broke in Noirmoutier. The car keys were in his trouser pocket. All he needed to do was pick up his passport, throw some clothes in a bag and leave. She would have found someone to bail her out, some guy; there was always some guy ready and willing to help. But he didn't go, he just lay there wondering why the woman he loved wanted to hurt him and why he continued to let her.

He didn't leave and then Easter rolled around again and Vincent decided, OK, one last time, mainly because he wanted to be with her family. He got a sense of belonging from her family, a feeling he'd never had from his own. His family never really felt like a family; they were just a bunch of people who happened to live under the same roof and were therefore obliged to tolerate one another. Ellie was Vincent's ticket into her family and he didn't want to lose his relationship with them, especially with Maggie who, for all her drinking, he loved dearly. But he was in no doubt that, if he ended it with Ellie, that would be that. No one had ever dumped her. There would be no mercy, no reprieve: he'd be out - ex, exiled, excommunicated, persona non grata. No one in her family would dare to have anything to do with him lest they suffered the same fate.

Brian put a Bothy Band cassette on, Tríona Ní Dhomhnaill singing *Casadh an tSugain*, the twisting of the rope, a song about a young woman who gets rid of an unwanted suitor by promising to marry him but only if he helps her braid some rope. The suitor agrees but the rope grows as they braid it and as it gets longer, they move further apart until the girl is out of sight, at which point she runs away. Ellie didn't know it then but Vincent was about to disappear over her horizon.

Remember when we saw the Bothy Band in Dublin that time? he said to her. It was a test to see if she'd respond, if she'd publicly recognise they had a life together. It was also a test of his resolve to end it all. True to form, she acted as if he hadn't spoken, like he wasn't there at all. He felt more resolute, but it hurt in the same old way. Vincent went back to studying the play of light on the whiskey.

What about youse, you and Vincent? Susan asked Ellie. Would you never consider tying the knot?

Susan couldn't get one over on Maggie, who was too sharp for her, but she knew how to get under her big sister's skin. She knew perfectly well that Ellie was opposed to the institution of marriage on principle, that it was an instrument of oppression and that a married woman was little more than a prostitute with a solitary client, but she'd never say anything of the kind in front of her mother, a woman whose life was founded on the bedrock of convention. For Ellie to say what she really thought about marriage, that it was a form of voluntary slavery, would be to insult her mother. Besides, Ellie – like the rest of them – was in child mode. She wasn't going to make feminist speeches in the caravan.

What sort of a knot would that be? she said, without looking up from her cards.

For a moment the silence was only broken by the click of Roberta's knitting needles and the pop and sigh of the ring-pull on a can of Smithwick's.

Well, what about it, Ellie? Vincent said, the whiskey running away with his tongue. Will you marry me?

Roberta stopped knitting. Vincent's words hung in

the smoke-filled air. Was it really a proposal or was he just messing around? Ellie turned over a card. Her mother looked at her but she avoided catching her eye. Maggie and Susan exchanged startled looks.

Now, Vincent, Roberta said, reprovingly. Don't be saying things unless you mean to say them.

Marriage wasn't something to be flippant about. She wanted to know if he was serious.

It's alright, Roberta. No need to book St Matthew's. On the ferry over from Stranraer, Ellie said that if we got married, even if we had kids, I could never be a member of this family, so there doesn't seem much point, does there? After all, that's half the point of marriage, isn't it, joining families together.

He said it matter of fact, as if it was no big deal, just one of those things, but he might just as well have laid a grenade on the table and pulled the pin. It was now up to Ellie to take the bait and either deny she'd said it or justify it. She sat, hands flat on the table, looking straight ahead at no one. Then she dropped her gaze to the cards and turned over a pair of jacks. Roberta resumed her knitting.

You're a part of our family already, as far as I'm concerned, said Maggie, managing simultaneously to smile at Vincent and sneer at Ellie.

Me, too, added Susan, more to annoy her sister than to mollify Vincent, whom she suspected of looking down at her the same as her sisters did. Roberta didn't join the chorus, however; she didn't say he was already part of the family. There was only one way in and that was marriage. Any other arrangement was provisional.

Ellie's family was her trump card and she'd thrown it away. At that moment when she said it, just before the ferry docked at Larne, amid the bar reek of chips and beer and warm plastic, something in him snapped, like a rope that has frayed to its last thread. She could go on raising the stakes, seeing if he'd jump, but he wouldn't, not for such small rewards. As they went down to the car deck he looked up at the bar – the metaphorical one – the one she kept raising, and said to himself: It's easy. All you've got to do is duck underneath it and walk away.

The Bothy Band played on to the rhythm of Roberta's knitting needles. Vincent tipped back the whiskey and got to his feet.

I'm stepping out to take a look at the moon, if anyone would care to join me, he said, looking at Ellie.

It was like a gun to her head. Come with me or it's over. She didn't look up.

You'll not see the moon tonight, it's clouded over, Roberta said, raising one hooded eye from her knitting.

Well, I'll take a look at the darkness, then.

He continued directing his voice at Ellie but she acted like he wasn't there and continued laying down the cards. He looked over at Maggie, whose eyes were swimming but she was alert enough to know that this wasn't just Vincent hurt and angry, this was something else. She gave him a consoling shake of the head and a sloppy smile. Vincent smiled back and then suddenly he started to laugh, not just a chuckle but full-blown laughter. Then Maggie started laughing too. It felt good, transgressive, like a private joke. Susan giggled.

Ellie looked up from her cards.

Would someone like to tell me what's so funny?

That just made them laugh all the more. Maggie snorted and spilled her vodka lemonade.

What in the world are you two giggling about? Roberta said.

Maggie snorted again and reached for the Smirnoff.

Vincent shut the caravan door behind him and stood for a moment on the step. Inside the Ford Escort, Tom was singing:

I've got a bad liver
And a broken heart
I've cried me a river
Since you tore us apart.

He walked towards the sea. The night air was sharp after the barroom fug of the caravan. The lighthouse beam picked out the flashes of whitecaps past the headland. He turned and looked at the lights of the caravan. He knew it was a last look, that this was it. He'd not be coming back; there'd be no more Black Bush and barnbrack for him here, nor more picnics at Ossian's grave or the rope bridge at Carrick-a-Rede. He'd miss it, the family, feeling part of something bigger, the drive up to the caravan through the Glens of Antrim, the road through Cushendall and Cushendun. But this time his resolve wouldn't fail him. He'd wait till they got back to London, then he'd tell her it was over. It didn't feel good but it felt right.

Vincent turned away from the caravan and towards the island, the sky, sea and land each a different shade of dark. He'd tried, he'd done his best. Ellie, too, he supposed, had done hers. You can't do more than that. Probably they could have done better, but they didn't and they were too far into the story to change the script. They were going nowhere, or nowhere he wanted to go.

He closed his eyes and breathed in the chill salt air. There would be recriminations, anger, loss, blame. He would be lonely, he'd have doubts, second thoughts, but it was over. He'd run out of road. One thing was ending, others would emerge, other possibilities, new loves, some worth pursuing. Who knows, perhaps even something not unlike happiness.